"It's over, Rico. I know the truth."

Rico's voice was soft as he questioned her. "What truth, Sable?"

"My father...you...the plans you made together. The way he offered me to you." Anguish sharpened her voice. "The way you tricked me."

"You're overreacting, *querida*," he said. "I simply took advantage of circumstances."

"You're devious and unprincipled, and I detest you! You didn't see me as a person—just as a commodity to be traded!" Her voice trembled with bitterness. "Well, you trapped me into marrying you, but I can't go through with it. I was out of my mind when I agreed, otherwise I would have come to my senses before...."

"Before it was too late?" he bit out harshly. "But it is too late. You are my wife—and that is what you shall remain."

ANGELA WELLS left the bustling world of media marketing and advertising to marry and start a family in a suburb of London. Writing started out as a hobby, and she uses backgrounds she knows well from her many travels for her books. Her ambitions, she says, in addition to writing many more romances, are to visit Australia, pilot a light aircraft and own a word processing machine.

ANGELA WELLS

WELLS

errant daughter

Harlequin Books

TORONTO • NEW YORK • LONDON
AMSTERDAM • PARIS • SYDNEY • HAMBURG
STOCKHOLM • ATHENS • TOKYO • MILAN

Harlequin Presents first edition June 1989
ISBN 0-373-11181-9

Original hardcover edition published in 1988
by Mills & Boon Limited

Printed in U.S.A.

CHAPTER ONE

HAD she been stupid to come here?

Sable glanced back over her shoulder, half hoping to see some sign of the extensive, white-painted *hacienda* from which she'd set out about fifteen minutes earlier. It was a vain hope. She sighed, angry with herself for seeking to boost her confidence in such a puerile way. The house was at least three hundred yards away and separated from the place where she now stood by a small plantation of citrus trees. Of course there would be no sign of it!

Shifting restlessly, she tried to pierce the darkness, her dilated pupils absorbing every scrap of available light. Nothing.

She uttered a soft, derisory laugh at her own predicament. Who would have thought when she'd first arrived at Porto Alegre, after the long flight from London, Heathrow via Rio de Janeiro with a chip on her shoulder as big as the Sugar Loaf mountain itself, determined to detest everything about this country and the unknown relations with whom she was to spend the next three months, that a mere four weeks later she'd be standing in the middle of nowhere in the early hours of the morning doing her best to ensure that her young cousin Rosina shouldn't alienate herself from her family as she, Sable, had antagonised her own father?

How much longer should she wait? Perhaps Aleixo had changed his mind? He was certainly late! Even if she'd had time to put on her watch it would have been of little use to her. The stars were bright points of light in the dark velvet sky, but there was no moon to help her vision. She shivered suddenly. Was it her imagination, or had the breeze taken on a chillier note? A stole would have been a welcome addition to her thin summer dress, but it had taken time to make Rosina change her mind, and in the end, once she'd got the younger girl's approval to abort her hare-brained scheme, there'd been no time for other than essentials.

Five minutes. That was all she'd give him. Then she'd return to the *hacienda* and the distraught Rosina and tell her Fate had made the decision for her. In many ways it would be a relief to be able to do just that. Sable bit her lower lip thoughtfully. It wasn't like her to interfere with other people's lives. There was a terrible irony in what she was doing, but against all the odds she'd grown very fond of Rosina—of all of them really, she admitted to herself—Uncle Roberto, Aunt Renata, cousins Toninho and Luis—and at just seventeen Rosina *was* very young. There might be only four years between her and her younger cousin, but they marked clearly the difference between a girl and a woman!

She started as a sudden rustling in the undergrowth startled her. Terrified of snakes, she consoled herself that the nocturnal prowler was more likely to be some species of rodent. She wouldn't panic. Rosina was depending on her. Five minutes, then. She started counting to three hundred . . .

'Rosina!'

She'd barely reached fifty before the sound of her cousin's name spoken urgently in a low, masculine voice forced a shriek of surprise from her lips.

'I thought you were expecting someone?' The hint of laughter in the voice did nothing to pacify her ragged nerves as Sable swung round in the direction from which it came.

He was some ten yards away—a dark presence mounted on a vaguely discernible equine shape. She narrowed her eyes, trying fruitlessly to bring him into sharper focus. Something about him disturbed her, was off-key, but the abruptness of his appearance seemed to have shattered her analytical abilities, leaving her feeling strangely vulnerable.

'I thought you were coming from the south track,' she countered tersely. 'I hardly expected you to creep up on me from the opposite direction!'

'Then I must apologise for frightening you . . . but there's been a slight change of plan . . .'

'Yes,' she agreed, experiencing a feeling of relief that there was no trace of anger in the quiet tone. After all, when a man had gone to a lot of trouble to plan an elopement with the only daughter of an influential neighbour, to have his stratagem thwarted at the eleventh hour was hardly conducive to a resigned acceptance—unless, of course, Aleixo himself had had a change of heart!

Sable took a few quick steps forward. What a weight off her own conscience it would be if independently Aleixo had realised how disastrously his plans could have affected both his and Rosina's lives!

She quelled the sudden rush of memory-evoked bitterness that rose inside her, but its presence lent her voice a carping edge as she stared up towards the paler gleam of Aleixo's face beneath the broad-brimmed stockman's hat. Stubbornly she fought down her premonition of calamity. 'At least you could have been on time! It would have served you right if you'd come to a deserted rendezvous! As it is . . .'

The rest of the sentence froze on her lips as the moon broke through the barrier of cloud, and for the first time she could see the face of the man she was addressing. Rosina had told her Aleixo was twenty and quite fair in colouring for a Brazilian, having blond-skinned German stock in his ancestry. Sable had formed her own mental picture of the young man, still at university, who'd fallen in love with her very pretty, charming cousin—and this was certainly not the Aleixo of her imagination!

For a start, the horseman who gazed down pensively at her stunned expression was no young student. The face was a man's face, late twenties, early thirties maybe, high-cheekboned, firm-chinned—a chiselled mouth, its purity of line heightened by the deep shadows beneath the lower lip and in the indented corners. His nose was classically straight, adding to the arrogant cast of his countenance . . . and his eyes . . . Entranced, Sable took a few further steps towards him until she was able to satisfy her curiosity. Deep-set beneath straight black brows, dark pupils surrounded by irises of similar hue regarded her with a mocking awareness that did nothing for her peace of mind.

Her fingers tightened against her palms, the nails sharp against the tender flesh. There was a legend in the cattlelands, her cousin Toninho had told her, about a phantom cowboy. No one knew whence he came or where he lived, but he would appear out of the blue, able to gallop dozens of miles in minutes, capable of rounding up an entire herd in an hour. Powerful bulls, it was said, remained motionless at his merest word or gesture. Women pined for him, but the mysterious cowpuncher spurned their advances, defeating his competitors in every other way before disappearing only to materialise once more many miles away to ride another range in his eternal search for his only true love.

The inside of Sable's mouth was horribly dry; her heartbeat thundered against her ribs, its reverberations thrumming on her eardrums; her voice choked in her throat, as every instinct warned her of danger. Of course she didn't believe in such bucolic fantasies, but whoever this man was, he definitely wasn't Aleixo—and that had to mean trouble!

'As it is,' he picked up her phrase smoothly, 'it's fortunate for me you were so patient.' She caught the white gleam of his smile. 'It's my proud boast that I've never disappointed a lady—and I certainly don't intend to do so now!'

Still shocked into immobility by the unexpected impact of his appearance, Sable tried valiantly to spur her mind to intelligent question. One moment the stranger was sitting relaxed, reins loosely gathered in his hands, then, before her astonished eyes, his body tautened as he spurred his mount into action.

She had time only to take one faltering step backwards before the space between them no longer existed and she found herself seized by an arm as strong and flexible as steel wire and swung up into the saddle, her body pressed hard against that of her assailant as his arm tightened cruelly round her waist, pinioning her into position in front of him.

Everything happened so fast, it was seconds before she could do anything other than grab at the edge of the saddle to steady herself. Then fury overtook any feeling of fear at her predicament as she threw her head back and screamed for help at the top of her voice. The arm that pressed into her diaphragm discouraged a further outcry as she attempted to refill her lungs.

'*Deus*! You have a voice like a foghorn, *menina*!'

'My father will have you hunted down by the police of two nations!' Sable shrilled angrily, turning her head, so that the breeze of their motion whipped her flowing black tresses against her cheek. She thought briefly with deep satisfaction of Jaime Guimares. She and her father had seldom seen eye to eye in the past, their angry altercations and bitter accusations spoiling any concept of the perfect father/daughter relationship—but the fact remained that in a fight there was no one she'd rather have on her side than her stern Brazilian sire, and Jaime Guimares wouldn't be sitting in London doing nothing when the news of her abduction was relayed to him!

'*Two* nations!' Her abductor's laughter was a deep growl in his throat, incensing her outrage further. 'I'm flattered, *senhorita*. You're obviously a prize well worth the having. And stop struggling or you'll have us both off!'

'I'm an excellent horsewoman,' she retorted swiftly, at the same time reluctantly obeying his instruction, since they were riding at speed over rough grassland and she had no wish to cause the animal beneath them to put a foot wrong and send them both flying. 'I don't know who the hell you are, or what you think you're playing at, but you're not Aleixo Covilha, and I demand to know what you've done to him and where you're taking me!'

'All in good time, Senhorita Guimares.' He leaned close to her so she could feel his warm breath against her ear. 'Delightful though I find your proximity, this is hardly the time or place for an explanation. But I do assure you, you have no need for fear or panic. We have only a short ride, at the end of which you will be reunited with Aleixo.' There was a short pause before he added, 'Unfortunately, he is suffering from a slight indisposition which has prevented him from coming here himself, but I can assure you his injuries will not be permanent.'

'Injuries!' Despite her assumed sang-froid Sable

couldn't stop her voice rising in panic, as a possible explanation sprang to her agile mind: somehow Aleixo's plans of eloping with Rosina had leaked out and he'd become the victim of his own plotting. The man whose arm lay so intimately just below her breast had incapacitated Aleixo, taken his place and, in the mistaken belief that *she* was Rosina, was in the process of kidnapping her for ransom!

Uncle Roberto was a wealthy man, his talents as an architect nationally recognised. To abduct Rosina from the streets of the small town near her home or from the campus of the college where she studied in term-time would be one thing, but to use her own rashness against her was fiendishly clever.

'Superficial but unavoidable, and as painful as they're inconvenient.' A note of regret entered his voice. 'I'm afraid you'll have to postpone your honeymoon for a week or so—how fortunate that patience is one of your virtues.'

'You devil!' Sable hissed the words at him over her shoulder. 'What have you done to him?'

'I? Why, nothing.' She winced at the air of injured innocence that cloaked his swift retort. 'Your lover is a very rash young man—he brought about his own downfall.'

Sable gritted her teeth, certain she detected an underlying current of amusement in the velvet tones. One thing was for sure, her original supposition had been correct. Whoever her captor was, he clearly thought she was Rosina. Not that the mistake would benefit her personally—her father could possibly outmatch anything his brother could pay in ransom terms, and once her true identity was established she would be acknowledged as just as good a prize as her cousin—but at least she would be a far more formidable challenge as a captive than the younger girl.

She bit back a wry smile, imagining how Rosina would be acting now had she kept her original rendezvous. The thought gave her an idea. It would be a mistake to show the extent of her own rebelliousness in the position she found herself. She would call on the experience of her three years at the Praxford College of Music and Drama to act the part of a young girl terrified out of her wits. That way she might be able to make her escape before her intention to do so was realised!

Deliberately she allowed herself to relax, as if her inner strength had suddenly departed, forcing herself to ignore her increased consciousness of the hard male body moulded so tightly to her own and the power of the strong thighs against the horse's flanks.

He was right in one thing. Now was not the time to continue the conversation further. Clamping her jaws shut as she controlled the burning indignation which threatened to make her break her resolve, Sable forced herself to try and identify landmarks as the journey across the rolling countryside continued.

'*Senhorita*—your ordeal is at an end. We have arrived at our destination.' Her captor was the first to break the silence between them.

They had entered private land some few minutes earlier, passing between iron gates in a high brick wall, following a winding dirt path to arrive in what appeared to be a stable yard. Dismounting as he spoke, her abductor held out his arms to her, inviting her to join him. A light glowed in the darkness of the stable buildings, increasing in size as a door was opened.

'*Senhor?*' A small, dark man hurried forward, bare-chested, fastening the waistband of his trousers. 'Is something wrong?'

'No, nothing, Eduardo. I merely had the inclination

to take an early morning ride. See to the mare, will you?'

'Sim, senhor.' Obediently the stablehand approached the waiting animal. Reluctantly Sable swung one leg over its broad back and allowed herself to be lifted to the ground by her abductor.

'Oh, dear . . . I feel a little faint . . .' She stumbled against him, clawing at his shoulder as if for support and allowing her knees to buckle as she swayed away from him. If she could distract his attention for a few moments, put him off his guard as she aroused his concern, it was possible she could make a dash for it.

Strong hands encircled her waist dragging her upwards. 'Just a few yards and you'll be reunited with your lover.' Dark eyes met her own, plumbing the depths of their innocent blueness as she matched his stare, seeking for inspiration. 'If it's the 'kiss of life' you need, then Aleixo is more properly able to administer it, is he not?'

The fiend! He was laughing at her, and for all he knew she might be at death's door, prostrate with shock and terror! She fluttered her eyelashes and groaned. Her heartbeat responded to her anxiety, sending a shudder through her body that couldn't have escaped his attention. 'If—if you could just get me a glass of water . . .' She made a determined effort to reach the ground, sagging heavily against the counterbalancing arm which still restrained her.

'But of course, Senhorita . . .'

Sable closed her eyes, expecting to be allowed to subside gracefully to the ground. Instead the next moment she was scooped up into a pair of powerful masculine arms and transported at some speed across the courtyard.

'Anyone would think you had no wish to be reunited

with Aleixo,' the pleasant voice of her kidnapper remarked conversationally. 'Believe me, he's going to get the biggest surprise of his life when he sees you!'

Furiously aware of the warmth of his arms beneath her thighs as he carried her into the hallway of a one-storeyed *hacienda*-style building characteristic of the area, opening the front door with a powerful thrust of his hip, Sable was forced to realise that he had sensed and dealt with her attempted subterfuge with a masterly perception.

There was one consolation, though. This arrogant soldier of fortune was going to get an even greater surprise than the one he envisaged for Aleixo when she, Sable, was presented to the latter as his fiancée! The prospect of seeing his face at the moment of disclosure almost made all the indignities she'd suffered worth while, she thought, as, holding her close to his own body with one arm, he used his other hand to turn the carved wooden knob on an imposing door at the far end of the corridor before kneeing it fully open and striding into the room with the air of a conquering hero. With a degree of malicious satisfaction, Sable's lovely mouth curled into a smile as she anticipated the shock in store for him.

'*Mai de Deus*, Rico! What have you done?'

The response was everything she could wish for as a young man, casually dressed in T-shirt and jeans, who had been lounging full-length on a large leather couch ranged along one side of the rectangular room, swung his feet towards the ground, following his exclamation with a yelp of pain, as the colour drained from his face. Quickly Sable assessed his appearance. Light brown hair, hazel eyes, an attractive yet still boyish face . . . this was surely Aleixo . . .

'Changed my mind, Aleixo,' the man she now knew

was called Rico replied easily, at the same time setting her down carefully, turning her so she stood with her back towards him facing the pale-faced figure on the couch, removing his hat and tossing it on to a vacant chair before returning his hands to the top of her shoulders.

'I was all set to do as we arranged—tell her that due to your mishap you were unable to keep your tryst, and advise her to creep back to bed before her absence was noticed, when it occurred to me that there was nothing to prevent my bringing her to you here.' She felt the movement of his hands as he shrugged broad shoulders. 'Since you're unable to drive, I shall take you in my own car to whatever hideaway you've chosen. There's no law that says a man may not marry the woman of his choice merely because he has been kicked in the ribs by a horse!'

A wave of relief surged through Sable's system. So this was no kidnap attempt as she'd originally feared! Merely an elopement by proxy, and one which had disastrously misfired!

Biting the corners of her lips to hide her amusement, she held her tongue, merely allowing politely raised brows to linger on Aleixo's horrified face. She'd find plenty to say when the right moment came!

'But Rico,' Aleixo spluttered, moving one hand to clasp his ribcage directly beneath his heart, as he rose with difficulty to his feet, 'that isn't . . . I mean, *she* isn't the girl I want to marry! She isn't Rosina!'

'*Not* Rosina!' The grip on her shoulders tightened as Sable found herself twisted round to encounter the blazing fury of dark eyes. 'Who the hell are you? And what the devil do you mean by masquerading as someone else?'

'Don't you dare speak to me like that!' He was the

most impossible brute she'd ever encountered, Sable decided angrily. Geared up to receive contrition, she found his tone of stricture particularly galling. 'It was *you* who mistook me for Rosina—I certainly never claimed to be her. She'd changed her mind about eloping with Aleixo and I offered to let him know so he wouldn't do anything foolish—like knocking at the front door, to find out what had gone wrong!'

'Changed her mind? But why? When?' Aleixo interspersed distractedly. 'God in heaven—has her father found out? Is she all right?' He made a movement as if to rise to his feet, but Sable forestalled him, shaking off Rico's restraining hand and moving forward to kneel at his feet so their eyes were at a level. Not for the first time did she begin to regret the part she'd already played in this drama. If it hadn't been for her interference in the matter, Rosina and Aleixo would be happily reunited and about to set forth to bring their marriage plans to fruition. Of course, she'd acted from the very best of intentions—and Rosina had been uncertain to start with, or she would never have allowed herself to be convinced . . . she sought to silence her scruples.

'It was a very sudden decision, you see.' Observing the unhappiness in the young man's eyes, she couldn't hold back a lingering sigh. 'Rosina was actually getting ready to leave the house tonight when she had second thoughts. She realised her father might never forgive her or accept either of you in his home in the future. It would be a terrible start to your lives together.'

'But she was so sure!' Another qualm of conscience smote Sable as the young man's face mirrored his confusion. 'It wasn't a rash decision. We've known each other for three years . . .' He broke off mid-sentence, gritting his teeth to conceal a tide of rising emotion.

'Oh, Aleixo,' her expressive face was alive with compassion, 'it's because she loves you so much that she wants time to finish her course at the college as her father wishes, before telling him that she's fallen in love with you. She hopes that you'll understand how important the approval of her family is to her, and if you really care for her you'll wait until the time is right to approach them. It's because she cares so dearly for you that she wants her family to welcome and respect you.' Her earnest gaze sought a response from his motionless countenance. 'And if you love her as much as I believe you do, then surely you won't begrudge her the traditional wedding and the send-off from the heart of her family that deep down you must know she yearns for?'

A spatter of handclaps from behind her made Sable turn her head.

'Bravo! A moving exposition if ever I heard one!' Dark eyes mocked her, and the slight curl of Rico's upper lip was marginally removed from a sneer. 'And are we to believe the little Rosina changed her mind at the eleventh hour all by herself, without any outside influence to unsettle her?'

'It's a matter of indifference to me what *you* believe!' Sable's eyes sparked fire as she confronted her questioner. She had influenced Rosina and there was no need for her to feel shame. Being in a state of hostility with one's family was no pleasure, as she knew to her own cost, and frankly she'd been horrified to wake up in the room she shared with her cousin to discover the latter on the point of making a clandestine departure!

'The fact is that Rosina *did* have second thoughts,' she retorted coldly, 'and because she was too distressed to keep their rendezvous and explain to Aleixo how she felt, I offered to take her place and explain the situation—only you never gave me a chance.'

'But you knew I couldn't be Aleixo. If I had been, I would have recognised you immediately for the impostor you are,' Rico responded, his voice equally icy, as he looked down his beautiful nose at her mutinous expression. 'I don't recall your remarking on the fact.'

'I *didn't* know you weren't Aleixo,' she fired back instantly. 'Not until it was too late to do anything about it. When you said there'd been a slight change of plan, I thought you were referring to my being there instead of Rosina. How was I expected to know you were referring to your own presence?'

A brief laugh greeted her outburst. 'Is that the reason for that ear-piercing shriek you let out? I assumed at the time you'd got carried away by the romantic nature of your departure and were overplaying your part . . . *Meu Deus*!' A sound of self-disgust sounded deep in his throat. 'Here I am, trying to play the friend in need to my young acquaintance, who was foolhardy enough to attempt to saddle up a horse an hour ago despite the doctor's warning that any undue exertion could result in his broken ribs piercing his lungs and prematurely ending his life, and I complicate his existence even further by presenting him with some empty-headed servant girl instead of his future wife!'

'I am *not* a servant girl!' Suddenly conscious of the fact that she was still on her knees, Sable rose gracefully to her full height, flinging her head back haughtily, allowing the dark, silken curtain of her hair to swirl round her shoulders as she bestowed a withering glance on the angry countenance that accused her of heaven knew what!

How dared he have the temerity to treat her as if she'd

engineered this whole occurrence, when he was entirely to blame? If she *had* been Rosina, his high-handed actions and lack of explanations would have terrified her young cousin half to death!

'In any case, why all the fuss? You've made a fool of yourself, but there's no real damage done.' Her voice faltered a little as she saw his dark eyebrows meet in a line of dissent. 'Is there?'

'That rather depends, doesn't it, my pretty one . . .' Rico's teeth showed brilliant white against his tanned skin, but there was no humour in that tigerish smile. 'On whether we can return you to wherever you came from without your absence being remarked on. I'm in no mood to have an angry parent descend on me with the intention of avenging his daughter's honour after her keeping what appears to be a midnight tryst with her lover!'

'Please don't concern yourself, *senhor*, on my behalf.' Sable's answering gaze was frigid. 'My honour is my own affair. All I require from you is that you extend me the courtesy of returning me to my uncle's *hacienda*.'

'Oh, dear lord!' Somewhere behind her, Sable heard Aleixo's voice strained and faint with horror. 'I knew I'd seen her somewhere before, Rico. She's Rosina's cousin from England! You've abducted Roberto Guimares's niece, my friend!'

'Is that true?' the tall, dark man who towered over her own five feet six inches demanded softly.

'Absolutely.' A whisper of pride echoed in her well-modulated voice. 'I am Sable Guimares, and I trust you won't antagonise my uncle by keeping me here much longer, now we all understand one another.'

Expecting instant action, she watched in surprise as Rico's expression assumed that of cynical amusement.

'From England, you say,' he mused. 'Well, it seems to me you don't fully appreciate the problems your interference has caused. But firstly, my dear Senhorita Guimares, allow me to introduce myself—I am Ricardo Antonio Macao de Braganza, at present taking a working holiday in this vicinity. And secondly—I'm afraid your—er—request that you be escorted back to your uncle's house forthwith is not such an easy one with which to comply.'

CHAPTER TWO

'IN THAT case I shall make my own way back without your assistance!' Tight-lipped, Sable made for the door.

'Senhorita Guimares, wait, I implore you!' It was Aleixo's impassioned tones that halted her mid-stride. 'Rico is right. You cannot just go back as if nothing had happened;'

'But nothing *has* happened!' Sable protested forcibly. 'Your *friend*,' she emphasised the noun, turning her head to glare briefly at Rico's grim face, 'acted irresponsibly, but apart from stealing an hour or so's sleep from me, there's no harm done.'

'If anyone has been irresponsible, it is you, *senhorita*, not I.' Rico returned her scowling appraisal with thoughtful contemplation. 'You come from England, you say? Do the English not have a similar proverb to our own, which suggests that where angels hesitate to interfere, a fool has no such qualms?'

'You condemn yourself from your own mouth, Senhor de Braganza!' Sable contented herself with icing her voice with scorn, controlling the urge of her palm to lash out at the supercilious face that continued to observe her as if she were some odd and not too salutary a being.

'On the contrary, my dear Senhorita Guimares.' His smile was a masterpiece of assumed politeness. 'I merely came to the aid of a colleague in distress. One is forced, however, to regard your own motives in seeking to prevent your cousin's elopement with Aleixo with some suspicion.' He paused while Sable hissed in her breath, before continuing smoothly, 'Were you perhaps a little jealous that, although several years your junior, she was contemplating matrimony, while you yourself appear not to have ensnared a suitor?'

This time she didn't hesitate, as his impertinent gaze rested on her ringless fingers. Swinging her arm back, Sable lunged an open-palmed blow at his mocking face, connecting with a satisfactory thwack on one lean jowl.

To her suprise and chagrin, Rico de Braganza smiled as he raised a lean-fingered hand to touch the skin which had flushed from the sting of her attack. She bit back the automatic apology which sprang to her tongue. Somehow she'd expected him to repulse her blow before it landed, leaving her with the credit of having tried to avenge herself without the guilt of success—but he'd made no effort to do so. Almost as if he'd intended to put her further into the wrong, she argued angrily to herself.

Not that she'd acted from anything other than what she supposed to be Rosina's best interests in the first place! But she'd no intention of explaining the background of her motives to the supercilious Brazilian whose own behaviour left much to be desired!

'The evidence of such a temper would appear to justify my supposition,' he returned languidly, apparently in no way abashed by either her verbal or physical attack. 'But, while I find this spirited exchange stimulating, it's achieving nothing. I suggest instead we all put our heads together to resolve this problem.'

Sable tossed her dark hair impatiently. 'Well, for a start, you can explain why it's so difficult for me to return to my uncle's house as I've already suggested!'

'Rico said something about you screaming when he collected you . . .' It was Aleixo who addressed her, re-seating himself on the couch and leaning forward, his boyish face anxious.

'Why, yes, I did . . .' Catching the sardonic lift of the older man's eyebrows, Sable paused.

'Her scream probably awakened the dead, but most certainly every watchdog in the vicinity,' Rico compounded her embarrassment. 'You can bet your life the Guimares household is in a state of uproar at the moment.'

'Oh, dear God . . .' Aleixo buried his head in his hands. 'This is going to be even worse than if our plan had succeeded.'

'So why don't we tell them the truth, if we're challenged on our return?' Sable spread her slim hands open, palms upwards. 'That Rosina and Aleixo were going to elope, but that at the last minute she changed her mind, so *I* took her place, intending to explain the situation to Aleixo, but due to an unforeseen accident he couldn't come either and sent a friend to explain to Rosina and . . .'

'Why not, indeed?' Rico's interruption was harshly abrasive. 'If it's your intention to put an end to all prospects of their eventual marriage, it sounds an ideal solution!'

'You mean my uncle would be vindictive?' she asked, amazed.

'It has nothing to do with being vindictive.' Rico heaved an impatient sigh. 'In this country men have a duty to protect their womenfolk. An unmarried daughter lives within the orbit of the traditional household under the aegis of the men in her family. If she misbehaves herself, allows herself to be seduced, then every man in her household has lost the right to be respected by his peers.'

'But that's absurd!' Sable retorted impatiently. 'No

one has the right to be responsible for another person's behaviour in that way. In any case, surely the whole point is that Rosina changed her mind? If her father opposed her forming a relationship, surely the news that she had second thoughts will only bring him relief!'

'You're speaking of matters about which you know nothing, Senhorita Guimares! And since I don't intend to give you a lecture, at this moment in time, about how Brazilian men see themselves in relation to their family responsibilities, I must ask you to accept my superior knowledge as fact!' The rebuke was sharp as Rico's jaw became taut. 'What your uncle's reactions will be if he learns of this aborted plan is something of which your little cousin will be well aware, even if you are not! And I doubt her second thoughts will dispose him any more kindly towards my friend here.'

'Oh!' Sable frowned, forbearing to comment on Rico's high-handed assumption of her total ignorance of the code of *machismo*. Didn't her own father adhere to the strict criteria by which a man was defined as being a man in all Latin countries? And hadn't she opposed what she saw as a harsh and demanding set of rules enough times, decrying its practice as archaic and out of touch with modern behaviour?

But this was certainly no time to offer her pithy opinion to Rico de Braganza. Especially since she had a nasty feeling that his own ideas on the subject might well be in alignment with both her father's and Uncle Roberto's! If she couldn't change the culture around her—what she must do was attempt to influence its consequences!

'You mean he'd ensure Rosina never saw Aleixo again . . .' She spoke her thoughts aloud.

Rico shrugged a powerful shoulder. 'I don't know your uncle, only what Aleixo here has told me of him,

but he would have many options open to him, *nao*? I
believe he has some influence at the Country Club where
Aleixo works in his holidays as a barman . . . what if he
should lose that job? Perhaps there is an older man he
would rather see his daughter wed—when he considers
her education complete. How long could your cousin
hold out against a determined attempt to see her safely
put into another man's care? Is your uncle a devout
Christian? Would he prefer to see his daughter become
a Bride of Christ rather than run the risk of her
attempting to deceive him again? Does he . . .'

'All right, all right!' Sable turned her attention from
the dark, saturnine face of the man taunting her to
regard Aleixo's troubled countenance, before returning
it to its original subject. 'I take the point you're so
colourfully making. But I can't see Uncle Roberto
forcing Rosina to marry anyone she didn't love—and
the idea of sending her to a nunnery is patently absurd
. . . but . . .'

'Yes, *senhorita*?' Rico quirked an eyebrow.

'You may be right about his trying to separate them.'
Her admission was accompanied by a sinking feeling as
Sable acknowledged her own implication in what had
happened. Rosina would never forgive her! 'Therefore
we have to make certain he doesn't suspect Rosina.' She
moistened her lips thoughtfully. 'I know!' Her
triumphant smile passed to the younger man's worried
face as inspiration struck her. 'If anyone challenges me
when I return I'll simply say I couldn't sleep, so I
decided to take a walk. I wandered too far, something
startled me and I shrieked and ran away and became
lost.'

'And how will you explain the fact that when the men
of the house answered your distress call, as they most
certainly will have, they found no trace of you, although

without doubt they searched the close environment on horseback, alert for just such an eventuality?' Rico quirked a dark eyebrow in her direction.

'Oh, that's an easy one!' Sable turned on him a smile that was as bright as it was insincere. 'I shall tell Uncle Roberto I was kidnapped by the "Phantom Cowboy of the Pampas", who shared with me one splendid hour of glorious life before reluctantly returning me to his doorstep.' She swept him a deliberately flirtatious glance from beneath her ample wealth of ebony lashes. 'I hardly expect my family would feel obligated to extort retribution against a ghost.'

'Only if they fancied they could trail the tracks he made and discovered they led to this place,' Rico returned laconically.

'Yes, I guess that could be a trifle unpleasant for you.' Sable's eyes gleamed with delicious delight. There was something about this man with his impertinent air and insouciant stance that was really getting under her skin.

'I was thinking rather of my poor injured friend.' A gesture of his head indicated Aleixo. 'While I am free as the air, he is rather hampered from escape by the same injury that brought about this fracas.'

Aleixo emitted a hollow laugh. 'I would have to hope the police got to me before Rosina's father and brothers,' he said sourly. 'Or my hopes of marrying *anyone* in the future will be nil.'

'Oh, this is impossible!' Sable was beginning to feel cold now, wrapping her arms round her own body to retain the remnants of its warmth. 'Anyone would think we were living in the past! I'm tired and I want to go back to my own bed!' She refrained from stamping her foot with maximum effort.

'And devil take the hindmost, is that it?' She found

herself grabbed by two ungentle hands as Rico barred her progress towards the door. 'Can't you stop thinking about yourself for just a moment? And as for living in the past, I might remind you that wherever you are in Brazil the past is never far away. In the Amazon region we still have men living as savages!'

'As we seemingly do here, as well, in Porto Alegre!' Defiance blazed from Sable's accusing blue eyes, as she left her tormentor in no doubt as to her meaning. 'And I would point out to you, Senhor de Braganza, that it's only because I *did* think about someone else, *Rosina*, that I'm in this mess now!'

She paused to heave in a deep breath. 'Personally, I'm not interested in your stupid country or its stupid traditions. For all I care, if it's going to remove suspicion from Rosina, everyone can believe *I* was the one who meant to elope. My back is broad enough to bear the shame!' Tears of self-pity glistened in her lustrous eyes before she banished them with a surge of will-power. 'It won't be the first time I've disgraced my family.' She met Rico's watchful face with an air of bravado. 'And it probably won't be the last!'

'Well, well, well . . .' His amused smile made her hackles rise as Rico took both her nerveless hands in his own.

For several seconds she looked at his bland expression. Oddly, the original impression he'd made on her wasn't diluted now that she could study him more closely. Without the stockman's hat to mask his upper face, she registered a broad, intelligent forehead and a head of thick, luxurious hair as dark and naturally glossy as her own. In any other circumstances, an unwelcome awareness warned her, she would have found his positive, very masculine aura attractive. In the present situation it merely antagonised her.

'Well . . . what?' she demanded irritably.

'I do believe you've come up with the solution.' Dark eyes passed appraisingly over her taut form. 'You weren't raised in this country, and it follows that your uncle will regard your behaviour far more leniently than his own daughter's.' He gave a shout of laughter, raising his chin and surveying her through narrowed eyelids. 'It shall be *you*, Sable Guimares, the liberated *Inglésa*, who stole out into the night to keep a romantic tryst with her Brazilian lover!'

Sable's doubt showed as she turned over the proposition in her mind. 'It could work,' she admitted slowly. 'But my uncle might still be very angry with Aleixo . . .'

'I think not, Sable Guimares.' Rico's eyes never left her face, drifting slowly down its pensive lines, appreciating the exquisite bone structure that gave her high, rounded cheekbones, a full, mobile mouth, and a rounded, stubborn chin with the hint of a dimple at its point, before returning to the blue eyes so darkened by apprehension that they appeared nearly black beneath the shaded light of the large room. 'Aleixo has enough problems already without looking for more! I was considering playing the part myself, since I was partly to blame for what happened.'

'I see.' Never had her feelings been so ambivalent. On the credit side, this arrogant scion of the de Braganzas was finally acknowledging his share of the blame, and his solution would absolve Rosina completely. On the debit side . . . Sable chewed at her lower lip contemplatively. However innocent she made out her supposed rendezvous to be, it was almost certain Uncle Roberto would feel it his duty to inform her father what had occurred.

Her father! Sable shuddered inwardly. Jaime Guimares would be furious when he was told of her supposed behaviour. As if there wasn't enough trouble between them as things stood presently! She sighed, brushing her hair away from her forehead in a gesture of despair, remembering his last exhortation to her at Heathrow—that she should treat the Brazilian sojourn with her relations as an opportunity to make a new start to her life, to put all thoughts of marrying Simon Layton out of her head, and to try and assimilate some of the ethics of her female South American contemporaries!

Now it would appear to him that she had taken his advice and deliberately corrupted it, flaunting her defiance in his face. In time she could tell him the truth, but not before Rosina and Aleixo had determined their own future. Until then she would just have to put up with her father's contempt. Grimly she acknowledged the fact that his opinion of her could hardly become much lower.

Damn all Brazilian men and their *machismo*! If she'd foreseen this situation a few hours ago she would have held her own counsel and allowed Rosina to make her own mistakes.

'Well?' Rico prompted softly. 'Why do you hesitate? Surely the worst that can befall you is to be sent back to London by your uncle? In which case you'll be only too pleased to leave my country with its outdated codes of personal behaviour, *nao*?'

Four weeks ago that would have been true, Sable admitted silently to herself. Now it wasn't. She'd found a love and warmth in her newly met family that she'd lacked in Jaime Guimares's beautiful but lonely London mansion. An only child of divorced parents, she'd never realised what it was like to enjoy the company of contemporary relations—not until she'd met Luis and Toninho and Rosina. The glitter of London suddenly seemed tawdry in comparison to what she'd found here . . .

No longer conscious of Aleixo's presence in the room as Rico waited for her reply, and unwilling to submit too readily to a solution which still seemed unnecessarily tortuous, she met his interrogative gaze proudly.

'I must admit your traditions puzzle me. In so many ways your country shows a remarkable tolerance to controversial situations like racial integration, yet it's so riddled with sex discrimination that a woman is still often considered to be incapable of protecting her own reputation!'

For a split second Rico's eyes swept Sable's stormy features, then he offered her a lazy smile. 'At any other time I'd be delighted to set you right on the principles of *machismo*. However, I'm still awaiting your agreement to my proposal.'

There really was no easy alternative. Reluctantly Sable gave a dismissive shrug. 'Whatever you think best—I won't oppose you.'

'*Obrigado—meu amor . . .*' Rico's slow smile was infinitely mocking as he lifted a hand to stroke the black silk of her hair in a gentle, possessive gesture. 'I anticipate our coming relationship with deep interest.'

As he bent his head, Sable felt the thud of her own heart and experienced a constricting tightness in her chest. Dear God, surely he wasn't going to have the nerve to attempt to seal their unholy bargain with a kiss?

She knew she was wrong the moment Rico's lips drifted in a casual caress across her forehead. Warm and firm, hard yet silky, they conjured up a deep, responsive shudder which erupted through her entire body.

'Trust me.' It was little more than a whisper from his

caressing mouth as he finally released her.

Trust! Sable turned her head away to hide her tumultuous thoughts. Simon had been the last man to speak the same words to her. Simon, whom she still continued to love and trust despite her father's fury. All she felt for this conceited Brazilian marauder was a deep resentment! Stepping backwards she made a point of passing her hand across her forehead, as if to erase the unseen mark he had left there.

'Supposing Rosina has already confessed her involvement in my disappearance?' she asked with one last desperate attempt to find an alternative solution.

'An unlikely occurrence.' There was a faint mockery evident in the dark eyes which lingered on her flushed face. 'I fancy your cousin lacks both your courage and resourcefulness—not to say impetuosity. And now, if you'll forgive me, I have to make arrangements to return you to your family before they call the police!'

CHAPTER THREE

GRITTING her teeth together as the harsh saddlecloth of her mount rubbed against her tender thighs, Sable rode in Rico's wake. Adamantly against returning to the front door of the *hacienda* by car as he had suggested, she'd insisted on going back the way they'd come, in the last desperate hope that her cry had gone unnoticed and they'd find her uncle's home in darkness.

Her full skirt tucked up between her legs afforded her a little protection, but in no way could it be compared to the comfort of riding breeches or even the thick denim she was accustomed to. Her discomfort was just one more black mark against the man ahead of her, who, suitably clad, rode with a graceful power that in any other circumstances would have won her approval!

'It seems I didn't overestimate the power of your lungs, *minha* Sable. Your uncle's *hacienda* is as brightly lit as the seafront at Rio!'

'Oh!' As Rico reined, she drew alongside him, staring at the evidence of activity beyond the citrus grove, feeling her heart sink. Seldom at a loss for words, she found that the prospect of making explanations to an irate Uncle Roberto was suddenly extremely unwelcome.

'Scared?' Rico's taunt brought the colour to her cheeks. 'Don't worry. Let me do the talking.'

'Sable? Is that you?'

Before she had time to reply she recognised Toninho's voice. Seconds later her cousin appeared out of the darkness.

'It *is* you, Sable! Thank God you're all right. Mama's having hysterics, Papa is giving Rosina the third degree and Luis had been riding around in circles for the last half-hour, while I've been searching through the undergrowth where a horse can't pass!'

Curiosity rather than annoyance was the dominating emotion on his pleasant young face as his eyes passed contemplatively between Sable and Rico. 'I'd say the two of you have got some explaining to do!' The knowing impertinence of his gaze didn't elude Sable or do anything to persuade her that the next half-hour was not going to be an unpleasant one for her.

'Certainly we shall explain at the right time and place to the right person.' Rico eyed Toninho with patronising tolerance. 'In the meantime the best thing for you to do is to find your brother and tell him the ewe lamb has returned safely to the fold, *nao*?'

Without waiting for a sign of compliance, Rico smiled reassuringly across to Sable. 'Come *querida*. Let's find your uncle without further delay.'

Roberto Guimares had never looked so forbidding in all the time she'd known him. Sable felt her heart dive alarmingly towards her midriff as she and Rico were shown by one of the Guimares's maids, who'd presumably been aroused by the commotion, into the small room he reserved for his own use.

'Are you all right, *menina*?' he asked gravely, watching her nod before turning his full regard to the man at her side.

'I assume, *senhor*, that you are somehow involved in my niece's temporary disappearance, and that your presence here is to explain what has been going on.' It was as if his whole body threatened as he rose slowly to his feet, addressing Rico. 'If it wasn't for the fact that my daughter told me she saw Sable stealing fully

dressed from her room, apparently intent on some
midnight mission, I would have called the police before
now.'

So Rosina had kept her own counsel, presumably
through fear of the consequences! Rico had been correct
in diagnosing her cousin's weaknesses. Sable swallowed
miserably. It wasn't that she minded taking all the
blame, just that Uncle Roberto looked so wounded, and
he was one of the last people she'd wanted to hurt. Still,
better her than Rosina, she comforted herself wryly.

'The fault is entirely mine, *senhor.*' Rico touched her
arm lightly as she would have spoken, implicitly
demanding her silence. 'Allow me to introduce myself.'
He slid a long-fingered hand into an inner pocket of the
black leather jerkin he was wearing, to produce a
business card. 'My name is Ricardo de Braganza, and I
have the honour of having recently met your beautiful
niece and fallen in love with her.'

'Have you, indeed?' Roberto Guimares took the
card, gazing thoughtfully at its printed surface, as Sable
gulped her surprise at Rico's choice of phrase. She'd
expected something far less bold. On the other hand, he
had no more wish to be implicated in this than she had,
and probably he knew the best escape route. She stirred
uneasily but remained silent.

Was it her imagination, or was there a sudden hint of
respect on her uncle's face, a slight lessening of the
righteous indignation that had harshened his expression
as he surveyed the piece of pasteboard in his hand?

'The Rancho Ribatejo,' he quoted softly. 'I've heard
of it. Cattle, I believe?'

'Prime beef.' Rico's dark head inclined in agreement.
'I'm staying temporarily at the Granja Branca, the polo
pony stud, a few miles down the road. It's part of the
Ribatejo estate, and the management wanted a full

report on its activities.'

'Yet you decided to concern yourself instead with my niece's activities?' Roberto's tone was stern but not unreasonable, as Rico faced him squarely.

'Senhor Guimares—I have been seeing your niece since our first meeting at the Romanes party three weeks ago . . .'

That was a lie, but a clever one! Nearly the whole town had been invited to celebrate the wedding of the eldest Romanes daughter. His assumption she had been there was quite correct . . .

'Tonight I persuaded her to meet me alone in the citrus grove to discuss our future, away from the distractions of the cafés and shops where we had snatched a few hours together whenever it was possible.' Rico smiled tenderly at Sable's stony face, before returning his gaze to Roberto's watchful countenance.

'When she agreed to become my wife, I confess I went a little mad, celebrating in my own fashion, whipping her up into my saddle and riding out across the countryside until we reached the Granja Branca, where she persuaded me to return her to your house.'

Marriage? There'd been no mention of marriage in the loose plan Rico had suggested! Sable stared at his smug face with angry astonishment, wondering how best to combat such an absurd suggestion. Obviously with the plain, unvarnished truth!

'Uncle!' she spoke for the first time, so incensed by the way she'd been manipulated that it was difficult to control her voice. 'I have no intention of marrying this man . . .'

'Without your approval.' Quickly Rico gave new meaning to her sentence.

'I have no authority over you, Sable,' Roberto said sadly. 'You're of an age when many girls are already married, and I have to admit I only knew Renata for a few days before I realised she was the girl I wanted to marry. But have you considered how this news might affect your father?'

'He'd probably be delighted!' The bitter words had left her lips before she'd considered their wisdom. 'Papa always wanted me to marry a Brazilian!'

'My brother only wanted your happiness, *menina* . . .' Roberto paused as if considering the prudence of continuing his admonition.

'In any case, it's of no importance!' Sable tossed her dark head arrogantly. 'Since I've not the slightest intention of marrying Rico de Braganza!'

'Without her father's blessing!' Again Rico had completely transformed her sentence, finishing it with a smooth aplomb that left Sable gasping with indignation. 'I'm sure I speak for Sable, too, when I ask your forgiveness for the disruption of your household tonight. In the circumstances, you'll appreciate my ecstatic reaction to your niece's decision.' He reached out, drawing her rigid body into his arms. 'May I hope that until we can make the necessary contact with her father and Sable remains under your roof, I may continue to see her, with your approval?'

'Uncle Roberto . . .' Sable began impulsively, then stopped. She was tired and wanted nothing better than to go back to bed. Besides, Rosina must be going frantic, wondering what had happened! And, however much she disliked Rico's ploy, it had certainly distracted Roberto Guimares's attention away from the original culprit!

In any case, Rico probably wanted to see her again even less than she wanted to see him! This storm in a teacup over, it was unlikely she'd ever set eyes on him. After a few days, when all this bother had died down, she could tell her relations that she'd changed her mind. That would be soon enough, or they'd be arguing here all night.

'Yes, my dear?'

At last she had a chance to speak—and realised there was nothing to say. Rico had said it all.

'Just that I'm sorry you were so worried about me,' she said helplessly. 'And I'll apologise to everyone else tomorrow.'

'We love you, Sable—and, like your father, we want to see you safe and happy.' He came towards her and clasped her warmly in his arms, before turning his attention to the man standing silently beside her. 'Senhor de Braganza—I can't say I approve of what has been going on behind my back. But bearing in mind the fact that you were obviously aware that my niece has lived all her life in a country where less regard is given to the proprieties we observe here in Brazil, plus the fact of your presence here tonight to explain, I'm prepared to accept that you have acted honourably towards her.' His lips twisted wryly as he held out his hand to the younger man. 'There's no doubt your action was ill-advised and caused a great deal of upheaval and distress to my household. Nevertheless, I was young once myself and I hope I haven't forgotten what being in love feels like!' Two masculine hands clasped in understanding as Roberto continued, 'As long as you have Sable's best interests at heart, you'll be a welcome visitor in my house.'

'Thank you, *senhor*.' Rico's dark head dipped as a noise outside drew Roberto's attention.

'That sounds like Luis and Toninho are back. I'd better set their minds at rest and let Renata and Rosina know that the emergency's been resolved.' Roberto passed a considerate eye over the couple before him.

'I imagine the two of you would like a few moments together before Senhor de Braganza leaves.' Roberto Guimares left the room, closing the door behind him.

'Well, I hope you're satisfied!' The latch had barely clicked before Sable rounded on Rico, her eyes blazing.

'Very much so!' He laughed at her outraged face. 'We've achieved just what we wanted, haven't we?'

Bridling at his complacency, she forced herself to keep her voice down. 'I can't think what makes you believe I wanted my family to think I was in love with you. I'd no idea you meant to take matters so far . . .'

'Why, for your own protection of course, my sweet!' Rico raised dark eyebrows patronisingly. 'We Brazilians are a tolerant people who smile at lovers, but have less regard for the promiscuous. It would hardly have been in your interests to portray you as a mindless flirt.'

'You have an answer for everything!' she snapped back, every line of her angry body ensuring he knew it was no compliment.

'I like to think so.' His smile was deliberately infuriating. 'I can't imagine why you're so upset.'

'And I can't imagine why you wanted to wheedle an invitation into my uncle's house. There's nothing here for you.' Her blood ran cold as she thought of the exquisite silver and crystal that graced the house. A professional thief allowed access could make a small fortune! Had she been set up for just such a nefarious purpose?

'Perhaps, perhaps not,' he shrugged lazily. 'But it occurred to me that I'll be able to escort you and Rosina to the Country Club now you and I are unofficially betrothed.'

'Assuming that you can afford the exclusive entrance fee!' she shot back, convinced that such a payment would be way beyond his capability. Membership fees were notoriously high, and far in excess of what she assumed a *gaucho* would earn. Scorn sharpened the gaze she turned on him.

'But I am already a member,' he returned mildly. 'Didn't I tell you that it was there Aleixo and I first became acquainted?'

Sable's breath hissed between her teeth, as she allowed her eyes to rove contemptuously over him, from the dark curling hair on his head past the soft leather jacket and trim waist to where his thumbs caught nonchalantly in the pockets of the close-fitting trousers that clothed his long, muscular legs before disappearing into leather riding boots. 'Presumably someone else sponsored you, *senhor*,' she averred disdainfully.

'How so?' He affected surprise at her conclusion. 'A *gaucho* might not be rewarded for his labours in direct compensation to the effort involved, but on the other hand the *pampas* is a vast and lonely stretch of God's country, offering little opportunity to spend what one earns.'

'Ah, I believe I'm beginning to understand . . .' Sable put her hands on her hips and met his amused glance, her small, pert chin raised aggressively. 'You saved your wages to enable you to purchase membership of a wealthy and exclusive club in order to further your own personal interests!'

If she'd hoped to goad him, she failed hopelessly, as he laughed. 'But surely that is what everyone does? You're not trying to make a crime out of it, are you?'

Sable shrugged, trying to hide her increasing irritation. 'Only if you use your membership to try and present a false picture of yourself!'

'You think I'm a con-man?' He smiled, but something in his bearing warned her to be careful of how she replied.

Tossing her head, unwilling to provoke him too far, but unable to deny his supposition, she compromised. 'I have no means of knowing!'

'Then we must hope you're able to find out during the coming days, when I hope to have the pleasure of your company in the beautiful surroundings to which you doubt my entitlement of sharing.' He gave her a small, informal bow.

'And I'm supposed to be grateful for such a privilege?' she demanded querulously.

'Oh, not you, *querida*.' He dismissed her interest with a wave of his hand. 'Even though it has the finest sporting and recreational facilities in the vicinity. But your cousin will be, and I think you owe her that. Have you forgotten that Aleixo is working at the bar there in his holidays from university? I thought it would be pleasant if they could continue to see each other in an informal atmosphere . . . that it might temper their passion with a little common sense. Or are you as opposed to their friendship as you were to their runaway marriage, hmm?'

'No, of course not!' she rounded on him fiercely. 'But if Uncle Roberto gets in touch with my father before we can put an end to this silly nonsense, there's going to be hell to pay!'

'I see.' He looked at her reflectively as Sable felt a spur of hope grow in her troubled heart. Perhaps this insouciant brigand wasn't as insensitive as he'd appeared, and was about to make some suggestion to alleviate the conflict in store for her? Not that she was afraid of her father, only weary of the continual arguments that seemed to plague their relationship!

The next moment she realised her mistake, as with a swift movement he grasped her in his arms, staring down at her shocked eyes with mesmerising intensity.

'In that case, *querida*, we'd better make sure you get good value for your money!'

His mouth sought hers with deliberate intent, the relentless pressure he applied forcing her to open her lips. For a moment she resisted, tensing her spine against him, but when he made no attempt to invade the inner sanctuary of her mouth beyond the limits imposed by her lips, she found herself relaxing as, inexplicably, a slow warmth rose within her, sending tingling messages of pleasure along her nerves to her brain.

Dear God! What was happening to her? Shame brought a burning patch of colour to her cheeks. Perhaps she *was* the wanton her father believed her to be! It was *Simon* she loved—Simon, the only man she'd ever allowed to hold her with such passion and to kiss her so warmly. Yet Simon had never conjured such a response from her as this arrogant stranger who had plucked her from the security of her family and was set to disrupt the peaceful holiday she'd been enjoying!

Sable tried to struggle free, but her effort was stillborn as, with devastating sensuality, his thumb caressed the silken skin of her upper arm, his lips continuing to tantalise the warm, rebelliously responsive curve of her mouth.

It was a slow seduction of her senses by a man experienced in the art, suspending her better judgement, persuading her body to abandon itself to the sensual pleasure of the moment. And it had to stop before it was too late and she reached her fingers into the thick, glossy sheen of his beautiful hair in an overt invitation for him to continue the uncalled for liberties he was inflicting on her!

Somehow she found the resolve to stiffen in his embrace, protesting through lips warmed by his impertinent behaviour. A feeling of total relief flooded through her as she felt his reluctant acceptance of her withdrawal.

Coolly he raised his head to gaze down contemplatively at her flushed face. 'You see what I mean, *querida*?' His eyes glinted wickedly. 'I believe you don't find me as physically repulsive as you like to pretend. Why don't we take advantage of the situation in which we find ourselves and have some fun together before your irate father demands your instant return to his side?'

How dared he treat her with such casual disregard? Drawing in a deep breath to control her voice, as she battled to regain her composure, Sable met his steady scrutiny without flinching. '*Why*, Senhor de Braganza? I'll tell you *why*! Because I find *everything* about you repulsive, and you've already forced me into an intolerable situation. Besides which, I happen to be very much in love with my fiancé and we intend to be married as soon as possible!'

'Betrothed to two men at the same time?' His eloquent eyebrows rose in assumed astonishment. 'I wonder your uncle didn't comment on the matter.'

'It's unofficial.' Sable's blue eyes darkened with contempt at his obvious amusement. She didn't wear Simon's ring, but she did have his pledge of fidelity . . . his promise that when he had earned enough to be able to offer her the kind of life he wanted for her, he'd return to England and make her his wife, regardless of any threat from her overbearing parent.

'Then he has my condolences, *meu amor*.' Rico's slow, sweet smile deliberately ignored her goad, although for one moment Sable fancied she'd seen a flash of emotion in the dark eyes that promised her no quarter. 'It seems you have an uncertain temper, a tendency to act without thought and a turn of phrase which might make a lesser man think twice before taking you on . . .' He paused as Sable's breath hissed in explosively. 'On the other hand . . .' his eyes moved in slow, thorough, masculine approval down the length of her body, while she stood in front of him, fuming '. . . you have an exceptionally lovely face and a body any man could enjoy, if he were able to still your tongue long enough to give it the attention it deserves.'

'Something you will never have the satisfaction of achieving!' Beside herself with fury, Sable swung up her arm, only to have it captured and firmly held.

'Not twice in one night, *minha* Sable.' Despite her anger, she felt herself shrink from the harshness of his quiet rebuke. 'I'm a tolerant man, but I warn you not to push me too hard.' His dark eyes seemed to bore into her very being. 'It's been an unusual night for both of us, but between us we've managed to save your little cousin's reputation. You may not wish to be my *namorada*, but there's no reason why we can't be friends, is there?'

He released her arm as he felt the tension leave it, apparently content not to receive an answer to his query, and made for the door, turning on the threshold to make her a formal bow. 'Until tomorrow, *meu amor*.'

As she watched the door close gently behind him, Sable's frustration threatened to choke her. There was a multitude of reasons why she'd never feel anything as tame as friendship for Rico de Braganza, and probably the most dominant one was that, in his strength of purpose and his rough-shod way of riding over difficulties and other people's feelings, he reminded her much too much of her own father!

CHAPTER FOUR

'SO THERE you are!' Rosina's pretty face was pale and blotchy, her swollen eyelids giving evidence of many tears shed, as she sprang to her feet from the bed on which she'd been lying, to level accusing eyes on Sable's concerned face as the latter entered their bedroom. 'Just what do you think you've been playing at?' Her mouth grimaced with scorn. 'Pretending to be my friend when all you wanted to do was meet your own lover . . .'

Sable passed a weary hand through her mane of hair. The night, or rather the early morning, had not yet released her from trauma. 'Darling Rosina, it wasn't like that at all . . .' she began, only to have her words truncated by her cousin's harsh laugh.

'Oh, don't try and lie to me, Sable. Papa's told all of us about you and Rico. No wonder you didn't make any objections when I kept going off and leaving you, saying I was going to do some studying at the library—you'd already got an assignation of your own!'

So that was where Rosina and Aleixo had hatched their plan! How stupid she'd been not to have guessed there was more than study on the younger girl's mind on her frequent disappearances. If she, Sable, had been a little less selfish, a little less concerned with discovering the secrets of her new environment, she might have been able to be a better confidante to the young girl who was regarding her with deep reproach.

'Listen to me, Rosina!' The sharpness in her tone was effective as her cousin clamped her lips together mutinously. 'It's rather a long story, so let me tell it first

44

and then if you've any questions I'll answer them.'

Patiently she related the events as they happened, starting with her first sight of Rico and ending with the specious relationship they now claimed.

'And Aleixo's not badly injured?' There was no sign of temper now on Rosina's pale face. 'He told me about meeting the stranger staying at the Granja Branca and how he was hoping to get a ride on one of the ponies. Oh, Sable! He might have been killed!'

'Instead he sustained a couple of cracked ribs.' Sable smiled sympathetically. 'He's seen a doctor, Rosina, and although he's in pain there's no serious damage. If Rico de Braganza has his way you'll be seeing him again soon at the Country Club.' She hesitated before adding warmly, 'I didn't have a lot of time to speak to Aleixo, but he seems a very pleasant young man, and obviously devoted to you. I'm sure he understood your decision. In fact, he was probably relieved his accident hadn't disappointed you.'

'But what about you, Sable?' Rosina asked curiously. 'I can see how it all happened, but how do you feel about Papa believing you want to marry this man Rico?'

'Resigned, I guess.' Sable wasn't prepared to divulge her feelings on the matter. Not that she could quantify them satisfactorily to herself at this early hour! Picking up her nightdress, she began to walk towards the en suite bathroom. 'I'm sorry you had so much worry before I could let you know what had happened. I did wonder if you might confess the whole thing to Uncle Roberto before I got back.'

'I was too frightened at first. I kept hoping you'd come back, and then before I could pluck up courage—you did! Oh, Sable!' She moved towards the older girl, throwing her arms round her. 'I can never thank you enough. I just hope this Rico de Braganza isn't going to make a nuisance of himself!'

A vain hope indeed, if she was any judge! Sable thought crossly as she splashed her face with warm water before putting on her nightdress and returning to the bedroom, where Rosina already lay on the borders of sleep, tired out by her weeping. Men like Jaime Guimares and Rico de Braganza were natural born troublemakers. She was as sure as she could be that during the next few weeks he'd prove her estimation of his character correct.

The only doubt was how? A slow shiver traversed her body. She knew nothing about him except that he was representing some cattle ranch on business. Had his willingness to help been solely based on his friendship with Aleixo, or had he some ulterior motive in obtaining access to her uncle's property? Was she to be his pawn in furthering some nefarious plan of his own?

It wasn't *her* fate that lay in those strong, slim hands, but Rosina's and Aleixo's. One word from Rico and the carefully erected curtain of deceit would be rent asunder, leaving the young girl who trusted her exposed to the wrath of Roberto Guimares. Yet if she continued with this farce of being in love with him, heaven only knew what disaster she might bring down on her newly found family!

On the other hand, she comforted herself, Roberto Guimares was no fool. He would surely check the credentials he'd been handed. In the meantime she'd just have to hope her 'fiancé' would get tired of teasing her, or that her father would surface from whatever business pool into which he'd dived and put an end to her supposed betrothal!

The cool cotton sheets were a balm to her tired body as she settled her head with a sigh on the plump pillow. How would her hubristic parent react when, for the second time in such a short period, he was faced with what appeared to be her defiance?

As sleep eluded her she found herself mentally reliving that dreadful day barely a month ago when in all innocence she'd confronted her father in his study with the news that she was in love.

'Love!' Jaime Guimares's black brows had shot up like twin bridges above the aggressive thrust of his nose. 'Then the sooner you fall out of love, the better!'

She hadn't expected him to fall over himself with pleasure, but neither had she anticipated the roar of disapproval that had followed her simple announcement.

'You don't understand, Papa,' she'd faced up to him boldly, 'Simon wants to marry me.'

'Does he?' It had been little more than a grunt from her stern parent. 'Then he's going to be disappointed. I've already made plans for your future, and they don't include your tying yourself up to some grubby little play-actor. I assume that's what he is?'

He hadn't had to be psychic to make such an accurate guess. Her social life outside drama school was non-existent, thanks to the sanctions he had applied to her since her return from an exclusive English boarding-school. Sanctions she'd never tried to challenge, content that she'd been able to persuade him to allow her to attend the drama college she'd set her heart on.

'Simon has just graduated from Praxford—yes!' She met her father's eyes with defiance in every gesture of her tautly held body. 'One day he's gong to be very famous. He's not only talented, but he has marvellous looks.' She forebore to describe Simon's Grecian profile, his mane of blond hair, his tall, slender figure, knowing they were attributes Jaime Guimares would dismiss with disdain.

As if he'd read her thoughts and reservations, her father had thrown back his handsome head and laughed, while she'd felt the blood drain from her body and her legs grow weak. They'd never been close, father and daughter. She at school, Jaime Guimares intent on his business, there had never been a free and easy communication between them.

It was as if his own unhappy marriage had soured him against all women, not only her mother, the lovely English cabaret artiste he'd met in Rio de Janeiro and followed back to London so many years ago. She, herself, had been barely two years old when Laura Armstrong Guimares had walked out with another man. Since then she'd been brought up by nannies, housekeepers and teachers. Somehow it seemed she'd missed out on love. Until Simon. Normally in awe of her father, this time she wasn't going to let him rule her life!

'Papa, please . . .' she'd begun, fighting back tears of frustration.

'So you've grown up at last, *menina*.' Jaime Guimares broke into her sentence with a smile stretching his mouth. 'Discovered there are better things in life than dressing up and speaking other people's words, eh?'

He continued, giving her no time for a reply even if she could have made her trembling lips form one. 'I always thought, if I let you have your way, after a while you'd grow out of this idea of being on the stage.'

'Oh, but I haven't.' She twisted her hands together in anguish. 'I mean, I still want to be an artiste like . . .' she hesitated, fearful of speaking her dream aloud, then, gathering courage, 'like Mama. That's why I asked you to let me have singing as well as drama lessons, and

I've . . .'

'Enough of this nonsense.' The smile had faded from her father's face. It had been a mistake to refer to Laura. She bit her lip in chagrin as he rose to his feet and came round his desk to stand in front of her. With unexpected suddenness his voice had gentled. 'My dear Isabella . . .' He alone had resolutely refused to call her by the diminutive of her baptismal name. 'It's a great mistake to marry out of one's class or race. I speak from experience, *menina*. Laura, your mother, was beautiful to look at, but she lacked the background and breeding I needed in a wife. That's why our union was a disaster.' His voice harshened. 'For thirteen years she denied me children. Then when, by a miracle, she conceived, she deserted both of us before you were two years old.'

Sable gave an uneasy laugh. 'Well, Simon certainly doesn't come from such a wealthy background as you, Papa, but we share the same racial heritage.'

'He's Brazilian?' The terse interjection shocked her.

'Brazilian? Of course not, he's . . .'

'Then he's definitely not the man for you, Isabella. In a few months' time I intend to sell up my interests here in Britain and return to Brazil, where I mean to introduce you to a man who will make you an ideal husband.'

Anyone else but her father, and Sable would have thought he was joking, but she'd seen that grim look of determination on his face before. This was no joke.

'You've *arranged* a marriage for me, Papa?' Her heart fluttered like the wings of a humming bird. 'But that sort of thing went out with the Dark Ages!'

'If you believe *that*, then the money I paid for your education was wasted,' he returned swiftly. 'A great number of caring societies protect the future generations by arranging suitable matches for them.

The man I have in mind for you is wealthy and comes from a respected background. As his wife you will have everything in life a young woman could want . . .'

'Including a career?' she flung back, hardly able to believe her ears at the plans that had been made on her behalf.

'Women weren't made to have careers. They were created to marry and produce children.' Jaime Guimares's face was white with anger at her rebellion, as he crushed the last vestige of hope she might have had, but she hadn't finished yet.

'And this husband you've chosen for me—is he young and handsome as well, Papa, tall and strong?' Her blue eyes had flashed her scorn at him, and for one sickening moment she thought he meant to strike her. Then he was moving away from her, returning to his desk, controlling his temper with visible effort.

'Physical attributes in a man are no guarantee of a good marriage, *minha filha*.' His voice was unexpectedly weary as Sable had stood there staring at him, her hands clenched against her midriff. 'I know well the man who is eager to become your bridegroom. Our families lived nearby when we were children. Eurico and I were good friends. We grew up together: spent our young manhood in each other's company—until we were both twenty-four; that was when I met Laura.' He paused, obviously finding the memories painful, while Sable waited, a dawning horror causing a constriction in her throat so that she couldn't have spoken at that moment even if she'd wanted to.

'Three years later Eurico married a beautiful Brazilian girl—Iolanda,' her father continued, his voice dark with remembered tragedy. 'She died a year later in the throes of childbirth.' He shrugged his shoulders in resignation. 'Eurico was devastated, but we kept in touch even though I was building up business here in London, trying to provide your mother with all the things she craved for. Time and again I promised to return to see him, but it wasn't to be until six years ago . . .'

With a superhuman effort Sable swallowed the lump in her throat, but her voice had emerged hoarse and cracked from its trembling column. Jaime Guimares was still an attractive man at sixty, but at twenty-one she'd no wish to marry one of his contemporaries!

'I won't do it,' she'd croaked. 'Nothing will make me agree to an arranged marriage.' She was shaking with distress because she'd never dared to speak to her father with such untempered rudeness before. 'It's Simon I love. Simon I mean to marry. I don't need your consent. There's no way you can stop me!'

'I can stop your allowance and I can cut you out of my will. If this young man wants you under those conditions I shall be very surprised.'

'I don't want your money—and Simon won't either—you'll see!' Disgusted that he should resort to such a venal form of blackmail, she'd turned and fled from the room, stopping only to fling a coat over her shoulders and grab her purse before making for the lodgings where Simon Layton resided.

After that, events had moved fast. Simon had been shocked at her news, suggesting that perhaps they should wait before rushing into marriage if her father was so opposed. Tearfully she had flung herself into his arms, telling him she didn't need her father's blessing. She'd marry him tomorrow if that was what he wanted.

It hadn't been. He had cuddled and kissed her, assuring her how much he loved her, even trying to force his lovemaking beyond the point where she protested. She'd always wanted to save her virginity for her wedding night, laughing aside his accusation that she'd been indoctrinated by her upbringing and the Church. She'd felt no need to be defensive about her decision. It was what was right for her, and she was going to make no apologies for being out of line with modern thought—if indeed she was!—and up till then Simon had accepted her decision with good-humoured tolerance. But that evening he'd acted like a wild man, only seeming to regain his composure when she'd shrunk away from him, terrified at his unbridled passion.

It was in a chastened mood that she'd returned to the Guimares residence. She'd expected Simon to be more enthusiastic about their marriage, but the lack of funds had definitely bothered him, despite her own optimism that they'd pull through somehow. Could her father's opinion have been justified? No, she assured herself. Hadn't Simon's frustrated attempt to make love to her proved how much he still desired her? If only she could have reciprocated! She'd wanted so much to please him, but everything had happened so quickly that, instead of responding to him, her body had frozen beneath his probing fingers, until she'd cried out in her distress and with an impatient sigh he'd thrust her away from him.

Afterwards he'd apologised, begging her forgiveness, asking for her trust. There would have to be a way they could wed without antagonising her father, he'd insisted. He, Simon, didn't want to deprive her of the life-style she enjoyed, and until his career took off he had nothing to offer her. Despite her insistence that she would find work anywhere so they could be together, he had been adamant. For the time being they should both keep a low profile.

A week later Jaime Guimares had summoned her once more into his presence. An evening newspaper was pushed towards her, one paragraph underlined. 'Unknown for part in new Brayne Temple series' ran the headline. A knife twisted somewhere inside her as she continued to read 'Simon Layton, a recent graduate of the highly regarded Praxford College, has been unexpectedly selected from a hopeful band of two hundred to play the supporting role in Brayne Temple's new series to be filmed on location outside Madrid . . .'

She hadn't needed to read any more. The smugness on her father's face was enough. 'You did this?' she whispered, knowing how loudly money could speak, and how diverse the contacts he had in the West End.

He nodded his agreement. 'Your *lover* came to see me.' He emphasised the word as if it was poison on his tongue. 'When he saw I was determined not to finance his affair with you, he named *that* as the price for leaving you alone.'

'I see.' Only pride kept the tears from spilling down her cheeks. 'What makes you think he'll keep his word?'

'Many things, *minha filha*. But in case he changes his mind I shall remove temptation from his path. I want you to go and stay with my brother Roberto and his family in Brazil for three months.'

'And if I refuse to go?' She sensed she was fighting a losing battle, but she wouldn't give in without challenging his authority.

'You'll find life very unpleasant. I mean to close down this house in the next week or so while I go away on business. There's an important takeover in the offing which I'm determined will go my way. In my absence you will have no means of support available to you.'

She'd swallowed painfully, cursing the fact that she'd always allowed her father to provide for her from his own funds, never thinking of asking him for her own

bank account. At the time she'd never seen the need for
it. Wisdom in retrospect was of no use to her now.

'Why are you doing this to me, Papa? Is it a sin to fall
in love?'

His face had the sternness of a stone statue. 'No, but
to be unchaste is. When Layton boasted about the
intimacy of his relationship with you, presumably under
the impression I would agree to your marriage on the
basis of it, he was lucky to escape with his life, let alone
the bribe he took from me.'

Nausea overtook her as Sable struggled for words.
'But, but Papa . . . he and I . . .'

'I don't want to hear.' A raised hand effectively
silenced her. 'The damage has been done. All I can hope
for is that during your stay there you'll come to your
senses: learn something from your cousins about filial
duty, moral ethics and mutual respect within a family.'

Her small chin had thrust proudly upwards as she
refused to be daunted either by her father's proposal or
his ready acceptance of her having anticipated marriage
with Simon. She'd thought Simon had known her better
than to have attempted to use that angle. He should
have realised how mortifying for her such a claim to her
father would be.

Yes, Simon was culpable, but he had lied because he
loved her. For her father to accept his statement without
allowing her to speak was unforgivable! Still, she
determined furiously, if he wanted to think the worst of
her, let him!

There was no trace of a smile on his hard face as he
continued, 'My brother suggested you visit him several
months ago, and now would seem an ideal time for you
to accept his invitation. Hopefully you'll be in a more
amenable frame of mind when you return. The only
reason I allowed you to pursue this hobby of play-

acting . . .' if he observed the way she gritted her teeth in frustration at his casual dismissal of all the hard work she'd put in over the past three years he ignored it with pointed disdain '. . . was because I thought you were too immature to settle down to married life—even though many girls of your age in Brazil are married with families. I see now it was a bad mistake. Not only did you meet a lot of undesirables, but it seems they managed to contaminate you with their amoral attitudes towards life.'

He paused, apparently waiting for her to defend herself and her friends. Instead she clamped her lips tightly together. Wasn't there a saying that to *excuse* oneself was to *accuse* oneself? Silence in this case was definitely golden.

Jaime Guimares had sighed. The exhalation of a weary man. 'Your promiscuity has shattered the hopes I've been nursing for the past six years. You've thrown away the prospects of a fine marriage, but at least it's within my power to protect you from fortune-hunters.' He'd gazed at her white, pinched face before adding more gently, 'You think me uncaring, Isabella, but consider—I waited thirteen years for you. Thirteen years of humiliation at the hands of a woman who flaunted her infidelities in my face.' His hooded eyes searched her face, 'As you know, our religion doesn't recognise divorce as ending a marriage. After your mother finally walked out she took with her the last opportunity I had for begetting more children. You were my only child—my only treasure . . .'

Had she detected a break in the deep voice? He only needed a background of violins to reduce her to floods of tears. But she mustn't let him play on her sentiment. Mentally she'd shrugged off the appeal to her sensibilities, trying to suppress the spontaneous wave of affection for him that had surfaced at his last words.

Her father was a tough businessman, too armour-plated to be hurt by any woman. If he'd treated her mother as a potential brood-mare, it was little wonder she'd left him and made a clean break, never divulging her whereabouts once the final decree had been passed. And as for the affairs he claimed on her behalf—she was hardly surprised that Laura had had to look elsewhere for the affection she'd craved. It was something her father wasn't very good at showing.

'Well?' Black brows rose interrogatively. 'What's it to be? A holiday with your uncle and aunt, or fending for yourself?'

If she'd been courageous she would have chosen the latter. But what prospects did winter in London hold for her—with Simon taken out of her orbit and job prospects in the career she wanted so abysmal? The truth was, she'd always had material goods lavished on her. To be deprived of them without any preparation was more than she wanted to face.

Was her father bluffing? There were dark circles beneath his eyes, a strained look on his face. A tremor of disquiet passed through her. She hadn't realised how quickly he'd aged these last few months. But he wasn't bluffing. The set of his jaw told her all she needed to know.

'Very well, Papa.' She'd been icily distant as she'd given him the answer he'd demanded. At least she'd won a partial victory. In Jaime Guimares's eyes Simon had dishonoured her, making her an unsuitable bride for his friend. That was one thing she could be thankful for! 'If Uncle Roberto is willing to entertain me—then I agree to go.'

Now, weeks later, stirring restlessly in her comfortable

bed, Sable cursed her inability to find the slumber that would put an end to her turbulent memories. She hadn't been able to believe in Simon's perfidy, preferring to lay all the blame for what had happened at her father's door. And she'd been right. Simon's defection hadn't been because he didn't love her—but because he did! The day following her second stormy interview with her father, he'd met her in the street and begged her to understand.

Everything he'd said and done had been for her sake, and when nothing had worked and Jaime Guimares had offered to get him this important role in Madrid if he would get out of her life, he'd agreed. And that had been for her sake, too. Once he was established the money would roll in and he'd be able to offer her the kind of life she deserved. He was going to free her from her dependence on her father for ever!

He had given her an address where she could contact him in Spain and begged her to write. He'd looked so young and noble, so like one of the young heroes he delighted in playing, that her heart had melted. Forgetting the rough way he'd handled her the evening she'd run to him in distress, she'd recalled only the gentleness of their previous courtship.

Flinging her arms around him, she'd promised him her lifelong fidelity and he'd pledged his own love in return. What was three months or so apart when on his return they would be man and wife? From that safe anchorage she'd launch her own career, attempting to emulate her mother's success at the top night spots.

She yawned as her eyelids grew heavier and her limbs began to relax. She'd written to Simon every week since her arrival in Brazil. Soon, soon, she would receive the letter from him she so anxiously awaited.

Even the disruption of her life by Rico de Braganza couldn't spoil the expectation of that!

CHAPTER FIVE

TEN DAYS later, stretching luxuriously on a padded sun-bed beside the glistening turquoise water of the Country Club's full-sized swimming pool, Sable reached for the long glass of iced lemonade on the table at her side. Drawing a refreshing mouthful through the straw, she allowed her eyes to linger on Rico's smooth body as he propelled it through the water with a lazy efficiency of movement.

Contemplating his dark head as he tumble-turned to commence yet another length in his economic freestyle, Sable tried to analyse her feelings towards her so-called 'betrothed'. The only concession she was prepared to make towards him was that she no longer suspected his motives in obtaining access to her uncle's household as being underhand in a criminal sense.

No, she rationalised, he'd simply maximised an advantageous situation for his own pleasure. Now he was sitting back and enjoying the hospitality of a local family and amusing himself with the companionship of their females. Not bad for a *gaucho* on a working holiday! Added to which, his sudden appearance on the leisure scene, she noted scornfully, had created a decided flutter of interest among her contemporaries, not to mention some older married ladies with too much time on their hands and receiving too little attention from their husbands.

If she were to be honest, she had to admit that Rico's presence in her life was as disruptive as she'd feared. In public he was a courteous and considerate escort. In private he'd left her in little doubt as to the low opinion in which he held her, proving himself to be as unsympathetic and intractable as Jaime Guimares himself.

'So you're determined to defy your father's wishes and marry this unofficial fiancé?' he'd enquired only the previous day, after he'd thoroughly trounced her at a game of tennis and they were walking back to the changing rooms.

'Of course,' she'd returned haughtily, furious that she'd been beaten so easily by his uncompromising game. She was considered to be an excellent player and a gentleman would have let her win at least one game, she thought illogically, infuriated by his callous display of superior male strength, which had ruthlessly probed her weaknesses on court.

It hadn't been the first time he'd questioned her about her private life. It was disconcerting how he possessed the knack of coaxing her into confessing some of her most innermost feelings, and galling to realise that after all this time ostensibly spent swimming and socialising he'd cajoled out of her many details of her life history—while all she knew about him was he herded cattle for a living!

'Of course,' he'd echoed ironically. 'Stubbornness is one of your least attractive facets, isn't it, Sable?'

'My friends call it loyalty!' she'd returned angrily, knowing that it would have been more dignified to have maintained a stony silence, but unable to do so, still smarting as she was from the pysical defeat he had inflicted on her with no regard to her pride.

'Something your father doesn't deserve, obviously,' he'd retorted drily.

'Not when his actions spring from an autocratic determination to have his own way!' Goaded by his

unwarranted interference, she hadn't been able to hide
the bitterness and hurt she felt towards her father,
aware that it was a painful relief to reveal the intensity
of her feelings rather than let them remain unspoken, a
caustic poison in her heart. Did he really think she
wanted to be alienated from the man who had given her
life if it could possibly have been avoided? Only her
conviction that Simon loved her and needed her, and
her gratitude at being the recipient of such total
affection, would have made her contemplate such a
traumatic break!

'It's not possible, of course, that his determination
springs from a genuine love and desire to protect you?'
Rico had persisted, unmoved by her distress.

'Naturally *you* would think that.' She'd paused at the
steps leading to the pavilion, to pass a scathing glare
over his unperturbed features, fully aware that, while
their battle on the courts had exhausted her, he, the
winner, appeared totally relaxed. 'I wouldn't expect
anything different from a man who is as rooted in the
same old-fashioned ideas and cultures as my father is.
But what I choose to do is no business of yours, and I
refuse to discuss my decision with you just because of
the false relationship we were forced to assume!'
Carried away by her own rhetoric, she'd added with a
toss of her head, 'I'm sure your opinion is valuable
about subjects on which you are an expert—cows and
suchlike—but I don't consider you qualified to offer an
observation on the way I choose to live my life!'

'On the contrary,' he had contradicted her gravely. 'I
can assure you my experience of the female sex extends
far beyond cattle, and you're far from the first
thoroughbred filly to show her paces off for my
delight.'

His mocking reply had incensed her. She hadn't

wanted to hear any more, but Rico's powerful grasp had restrained her as she would have swept past him.

'You're no tragic heroine, Sable Guimares,' he had told her roughly, 'cast out into the cruel world by an uncaring parent. You're the extremely spoilt daughter of a man with more money than sense!'

'So you're not a social climber, after all . . .' she'd flung back at him.

A wave of warmth passed over her cheeks now as she recollected her rudeness. Not that he hadn't deserved it, she consoled herself, closing her eyes and blotting out his real image as she recalled the response her smart retort had evoked.

'I'm a man who believes that beauty is nothing in a woman unless it's accompanied by consideration for her fellow creatures!' His hand on her arm tightened as he glared down at her. 'You can thank your lucky stars that I'm not your father. I can assure you I'd have been far less tolerant of your tantrums!'

Tantrums! She'd choked angrily at his scathing condemnation. The one thing she hadn't confided in Rico was Jaime Guimares's original intention of marrying her off to his wealthy boyhood friend. Somehow such a confession would have been too humiliating to make to this dark-eyed stranger who was intent on aggravating her. Perhaps if he'd known he would have been more sympathetic to her rebellion. On second thoughts, there had been nothing in his taut face to suggest he was prepared to give her the smallest quarter, whatever alleviating factor she produced to justify her determination to marry a man her father despised. 'Oh, I do,' she'd returned sweetly when she'd got her breath back. 'The thought of you as a father is terrifying!'

'Even more so than as a husband?' he had enquired

blandly.

'A thought of nightmare propensity!' She had stared pointedly at his hand on her arm. 'I'd appreciate your letting me go to the shower now, if you've quite finished with me.'

'Why not?' The question was rhetorical as his grasp loosened and she was able to free her arm, rubbing it with a dramatic show of discomfort intended to shame him, but obviously failing to do so as a slow, humourless smile curved his mouth. 'I haven't quite finished with you yet, but you certainly do need a shower.' His eyes had passed in impersonal assessment over her flushed face and panting body. 'And don't look so distressed, Sable; you can't win every game you play, and a good male player will always beat a good female player—unless he gives her concessions.'

'And they're something I can never expect from you!' She'd brushed past him, throwing the remark back over her shoulder, wondering why she should allow herself to be so irritated by his disapproval. Heaven knew, Rico de Braganza meant nothing to her. In a few days' time, when his holiday ended or her father intervened, she would be shot of him for ever!

'Why should you?' His answer had echoed in her ears as she'd let the swing door close behind her. 'Isn't the silver spoon in your mouth concession enough?'

Twenty-four hours later the words still rankled, as did his assumption that she'd minded losing to him at tennis. Of course, what he'd said had been right and she hadn't really expected to beat him, only to put up a much better show. After all, she had been coached in the game, while he had surely not had much opportunity for practice out in the wilds. Even then, it wasn't what he had done, but the way he had systematically and cruelly demolished her game as if he had been administering a punishment, that had peeved her. How dared he sit in judgement over her?

If only she could to call his bluff by announcing to Uncle Roberto that she'd changed her mind about marriage, but she must consider Rosina. She must try to keep her relationship with Rico on a civil basis until he acknowledged that their masquerade could end. The younger girl, she allowed helplessly, thought Rico was wonderful. Naturally her cousin would approve wholeheartedly of the man who made her continued contact with Aleixo so easy. With her father and elder brothers so intent on their careers that they had little time left for relaxing in the luxurious confines of the Club, and with her mother uninterested in the pleasures it could offer, if it hadn't been for Rico she would have been forced to continue her rare and clandestine meetings with the young student, instead of speaking to him openly in a recognised social venue.

Despite his injury, which was fortunately improving rapidly, Aleixo had managed to continue working, and Rosina was positively glowing with happiness in his company. Hopefully, when this masquerade was ended, her cousin would be able to find some means of persuading her father to accept Aleixo—if not as a prospective husband—at least as one of her friends!

In the meantime she, Sable, would have to maintain a veneer of civilisation in Rico's company, however much his company made her emotions churn.

'Not swimming today, Sable?' Rico's deep voice so close to her made her start. She must have been daydreaming for longer than she'd supposed.

She stretched lazily. 'Not for the moment—perhaps later. I'm too comfortable where I am.'

She pulled the sun-bed up into a semi-reclining position as he picked up his towel from an adjacent chair and began to dry himself. Stripped, he was magnificent, she accorded dispassionately. Thankful that behind her dark glasses the direction of her gaze would go undetected, she allowed her eyes to dwell on him. It wasn't, she decided, as if she'd never seen a man half-naked before. Simon had been only too keen to parade his weight-trained body before her, flexing his muscles for her to admire.

The difference between the two men was that Rico's body was almost certainly the product of labour as opposed to deliberate training, the muscles beneath the satin skin formed and perfected by natural exercise. This was how Man the Hunter had been designed to look—lean and powerful and lethal. She didn't have to like him to admit that he was an extremely attractive man.

'How much longer are you staying at the Granja Branca?' she asked indolently as having dried off to his own satisfaction he spread himself out on the lounger beside her.

'Until the work I have to do is finished.' His reply was as casual as her question. 'Why? Are you so anxious to be rid of me?'

She shrugged, not wishing to acknowledge the truth of his assertion. 'I just wondered. You can't have done much work these past days. You've spent most of your time lazing around here or being entertained by my uncle and aunt!'

'And you object to that?' he asked swiftly, a slight edge to his voice.

'No, of course not. It's natural in the odd circumstances in which we find ourselves, but your boss at the Rancho Ribatejo might if he found out!'

'Don't worry your beautiful head about it, *querida*. I can assure you he trusts me,' came the laconic reply.

'Besides, I *am* working. Sometimes to three or four in the morning. I find it the best time to go over the books, when everything is still and quiet.'

'Books!' Sable was startled out of her sun-induced lethargy. 'But I assumed you were checking on practicalities—like stabling and feeding and training—not bookkeeping!'

She was rewarded by a sharply perceptive glance from Rico's dark eyes.

'There's something bothering you?' he enquired sweetly.

'Only that it seems a little odd for a *gaucho* to be dispatched to do an audit!'

'Ah . . .' He swung round on the lounger, placing his feet on the ground and resting his elbows on his knees, supporting his chin on his clenched hands. 'I see you doubt my mathematical ability for such a purpose. But then, I never claimed to be only a *gaucho*. I merely told your uncle I worked at the Rancho Ribatejo and that we maintained a herd of prime beef cattle.'

'But you implied . . .' Sable broke off her sentence in confusion. She couldn't pinpoint the precise occasions, but she knew he'd deliberately led her to believe he was a working stockman. His conversation over the past few days had been threaded with allusions to the rolling *pampas* and life in the saddle.

'On the contrary, *minha* Sable,' he corrected her gently. 'It was you who jumped to the conclusion that my brawn outweighed my brain, and insisted on treating me as if I had no life out of the saddle.'

Warm colour flooded her cheeks beneath his amused appraisal. Had she really been so much at fault? True, she had never enquired into his personal life, since she'd seen it as of no importance to her. She bit her lip as yet another explanation hit her. Had she perhaps been

influenced by his first dramatic appearance into her life
and subconsciously cast him into the romantic role of
the Phantom Cowboy? If so, she'd been unimagineably
crass!

'But you did nothing to disillusion me . . .' she
protested.

'Why should I have?' he asked her mildly. 'Your
simple assumptions amused me. Besides, basically I *am*
a *gaucho*. My work centres round the Rancho Ribatejo
in the far south of the State. It's a large ranch, although
not the largest in Brazil. We run fifty thousand head of
prime beef cattle.' He paused, then smiled at Sable's
rapt expression and her quick nod, inviting him to
continue.

'That in itself is rather unusual, since most of the
ranches run a hardier strain crossed with Zebu stock
bought in from India to withstand the rigours of a sub-
tropical climate! But at Ribatejo the climate is
temperate and for the past few years we've been
carrying out a plan to improve the pastures. Acres and
acres of the ground have been ploughed and re-sown
with good quality grass seed.'

'Re-seeding the *pampas*?' Sable asked faintly,
astonished by the size of the spread with which he was
associated, and intrigued to learn more. 'That sounds
like trying to fill the ocean with a teaspoon!'

Her enquiring blue eyes were rewarded with a smile
and a soft chuckle. 'It's not done by hand, *querida*. We
use small aircraft to distribute the seed.' He leant
forward slightly, a mocking acknowledgement of her
ignorance showing in his smiling eyes. 'We're not
talking about an English back garden, *meu amor*. We're
speaking of an area where land is measured in leagues
and a field of two hundred acres is nothing but a small
paddock, and a man may ride for a week and never see

another living soul.'

'You sound as if you love your work.' Behind the patina of civilisation Sable had sensed that same reckless presence she'd first identified the night of their first eventful meeting. In the faraway look of his eyes and the wistfulness in his deep voice she recognised a longing to return to the extensive grasslands. An answering curiosity stirred within her, as she imagined the wide open spaces beneath the scorching sun, and the quiet nights with their shining stars.

Rico tossed her a rueful smile. 'I was born to it, and leave it as I must, there always comes the time when it calls me back. We have a word here in Brazil for such a feeling—*saudade*. A mixture of nostalgia and yearning and something still again which is difficult to put into other words.' His brilliant eyes clouded as she gazed into their depths, mesmerised by what he was divulging. 'I only wish my father was still alive to see the improvements we've made in the last few years.'

'Your father? Did he work there, too?'

For a moment Sable thought he was too lost in memories to have heard her question, and was on the point of repeating it, when he said simply, 'My father owned Ribatejo. On his death it became my responsibility.'

It was a few seconds before the full import of his casual words struck home. When they did, Sable eyed him warily across the small table between them.

'You're telling me *you* own a cattle ranch?' Disbelief seared the question. He had to be teasing her!

'Yes.' The bland monosyllable did little to dispel her misgivings.

'With fifty thousand head of cattle?'

'Give or take a couple of hundred.' Rico was watching her with quiet amusement evident on the lean planes of his face.

It was not a humour she could find it in herself to echo. He'd made a complete fool of her! She recalled with a bitter sense of shame the way she had patronised him on their first visit to the Club, her overbearing attitude only diminishing when it had become perfectly clear that he was more at home there with its customs than she herself . . . Dear God! How he must have laughed at her behind her back!

'How dare you try and fool me?' Anger rose to cover her embarrassment. 'The least you could have done was to tell me the truth!'

'Why?' He mocked her. 'I didn't think your ego needed any boosting, *querida*. To be honest I thought it might teach you a little humility to find yourself betrothed to a lowly *gaucho*.'

The colour in her cheeks echoed the flaming hibiscus print that covered her heaving breasts. Now he was accusing her of being a snob, and that had never been true! If she'd objected to his name being linked with her own so arbitrarily, it had been because of his arrogant behaviour, not because of his calling! Sable gritted her teeth, determined not to attempt an explanation.

'Besides,' Rico continued mildly, 'as I said, I *am* a gaucho. Many's the time I've ridden the range with my men, eating and sleeping rough.' His expression sobered. 'I was twenty-four, with a reputation for being a little wild, when my father died. Of course there were plenty of people employed to help and guide me, but mine was the final authority and I sensed there were those among them who doubted my ability to handle such a responsibility. They had to be shown I could. And the only way to do that was to win their respect: show them I wasn't prepared to ask of them anything I couldn't do myself.'

'But—but . . .' Sable stammered, still shocked by his revelation, and angry at his original silence. 'In the circumstances you owed it to me to tell me the truth!' If she was being unreasonable she refused to admit it!

'Really?' Rico murmured, lifting his eyebrows in an elegant expression of astonishment. 'I wasn't under the impression I owed you anything. If it hadn't been for my stepping in to help you, you'd be carrying the burden of Rosina's broken romance on your lovely shoulders, *nao*? Although perhaps I would have enlightened you,' he mused softly, 'if you'd ever shown the slightest sign of wanting to know anything at all about me, but until today there was no sign of that.' His beautiful mouth widened into a wicked grin. 'On the other hand, perhaps I was hoping you would grow to like me for myself rather than my possessions.'

'Well, I could hardly have expected you had any position of authority after the way you behaved,' Sable defended herself hotly, stung by his reference to her possible venality, and deciding to ignore his previous sarcasm. 'Galloping off with me as you did was totally irresponsible.'

'A throwback to my wild past, no doubt.' Rico nodded his dark head agreeably. 'But I can't say I regret it.' He cast her an appraising look. 'As a matter of fact there's quite a history of elopement in our family. My cousin waylaid his wife when she was on her way to become another man's bride, and *his* grandfather stole away with his boss's daughter one dark night when her father's back was turned.'

'Is that supposed to excuse your own recklessness?' She didn't wait for a reply. Fifty thousand head of prime beef cattle! Dear heavens, the man was a maverick! Angrily she rose to her feet. Standing still and beautiful in the showy one-piece costume with its low-laced front and back curving to below her waist, high-cut legs displaying her own lengthy golden limbs to their fullest advantage, she gazed down haughtily at the man still seated. 'I'm going in to the bar to find Rosina. I fancy a change of company.'

'I'll join you, then. I feel the same way.' He was on his feet, towering over her, silver-striped bathing shorts flattering without defining the muscled power of his male anatomy.

Useless to insist that she wanted to go somewhere without him in attendance. Confused by his deliberate deception, she needed to be somewhere quiet to come to terms with the cavalier way in which her intelligence had been insulted. Not many people had made a fool of Sable Guimares, and his accomplishment in doing so rankled! A sudden thought struck her.

'Does Uncle Roberto know who you are?' she demanded peremptorily.

'Why so angry, Sable? Mmm?' His smile infuriated her. 'You were in the room when I handed him my card, *nao*?'

Yes, she had been, and assumed it was merely accrediting him to the ranch, not declaring him as its owner. No wonder Uncle Roberto had been so kindly inclined towards him—the camaraderie of the monied classes was a powerful freemasonry, she accorded bitterly.

Raising accusing eyes to his bland countenance, stung by his condescending attitude, suddenly something snapped inside her. They were both standing a foot or so away from the pool edge, but while Sable's curvaceous body was held rigid with indignation, Rico's powerful frame was gracefully relaxed as he faced her, the corners of his mouth twitching at her discomfiture. Not stopping to think twice, she lunged forward towards him, hands outstretched, both her palms aimed for his lean midriff. The result was inevitable. Marginally too slow to read her purpose, Rico staggered back under her assault and landed with a tremendous splash in the deep end.

She paused for a mere second, watching him jack-knife in the water and rise to the surface shaking the water from his eyes and mouth, before thrusting her bare feet in sandals and reaching for the colourful *pareo* which matched her swimsuit. That, at least, had taken the smile from his face! Jauntily she began to walk towards the main bar of the complex, knotting the *pareo* on one shoulder and round her waist to conform with the Club's dress regulations.

It must have been a sixth sense that warned her to look round when she'd barely covered half the distance to her destination. A curl of apprehension ran through her as she saw Rico advancing on her, still clad only in bathing shorts, his bare feet covering the ground between them with alarming speed. It wasn't so much the speed of his stride as the narrowed intensity of his dark eyes and the dangerous smile that curved his mouth that promised her no good.

Certain he was seeking retribution for his unceremonious ducking, and with no wish to be carried back to the pool and made an exhibition of, she began to run. Yards away from the entrance to the Club, she glanced once more over her shoulder. He was still advancing on her, his expression malevolent to say the least. Damn the man! She wouldn't put it past him to make a scene in front of Rosina, and there was no saying what kind of embarrassing retribution he might have in store for her.

On impulse she turned away from the main club building, heading instead for the golf course. Here, in

the thickly wooded environs, she could possibly elude
Rico until his temper had cooled to match his body
temperature! She repressed a giggle, remembering how
comical he had looked as his unsuspecting body had
flailed into the water.

Running freely, confident of her own speed and
agility and the advantage she possessed by wearing
sandals, she was soon weaving in and out of the
specially planted and watered lush vegetation,
eventually sinking down on a fallen tree trunk to regain
her breath. She was alone. Not a sound disturbed the
early afternoon silence, certainly not the sound of
anyone crashing through the foliage in her wake.
Smugly she congratulated herself on outdistancing
Rico. Probably by now he'd retraced his steps, collected
some decent wearing apparel and was restoring his
injured ego in the bar.

'What a pleasant place for a picnic!' The deep,
familiar voice immediately behind her had Sable
jumping to her feet in alarm and twisting round to face
him.

'Rico!' she gasped, shocked out of her complacency
by the gleam in his dark eyes and the determined slant to
his strong mouth. 'I didn't expect you to follow me
here!'

'Didn't you?' he grinned at her, his teeth sparkling
white against the tanned skin. 'You were as easy to track
as a brightly coloured butterfly among all this greenery.
You surely didn't think I'd let you escape without
exacting payment for your amusement?'

She shrugged with less concern than she was feeling.
'Surely you're big enough to take a joke?'

He nodded, holding his distance only a couple of feet
in front of her. 'And more than big enough to repay it in
kind.'

He took a step towards her and now he was so close she could smell the clean, tangy scent of the pool-water on his still damp skin. Despite herself she shivered, her head turning in panic to see if her way to flight lay clear, as her heart thudded with alarm.

'Ah, no, *meu amor*.' He had discerned her quick movement. 'You can't run from me. I could have overtaken you at any time I liked, but it suited me fine to see you making for the lake.'

'The lake!' Her eyes widened. Of course, she'd forgotten the large man-made lake which was a central feature of the course. A qualm of real fear tingled through her veins. Unlike the pool, the lake water would be cold and dirty, its banks rough and its depths a mass of tangled weed. She swallowed nervously, all thought of antagonising him further dying from her mind.

'Rico—you wouldn't,' she began breathlessly, raising her eyes beseechingly towards him as he reached towards her, seizing her arms.

'Not when there's another alternative . . .' he agreed softly, his mouth claiming hers in a kiss that married passion to punishment and left her gasping.

Sensation streamed through her veins as her hot, oiled skin was drawn into intimate contact with Rico's cool, damp flesh. When he raised one hand to her shoulder to unknot the *pareo*, she made no attempt to stop him. Then his cool fingers were drawing the vivid material down her body.

Before she realised what was happening she became aware of the rough texture of the grass beneath her back as Rico eased her down, following the passage of her body with his own. Dark hair spilling on the ground, in that instant Sable forgot the outrage she had felt against him, knowing only the present pleasure of his mouth against her own and the erotic touch of his fingers against her breast.

Tenderly he used his superior strength to plunder her mouth with a slow eroticism, persuading her soft lips to open and receive his deepening caresses, as she responded mindlessly to the urgency of his demands.

Oblivious to anything but the taut, hard male form which pressed her softer shape against the unyielding ground, Sable found herself relaxing, accepting and enjoying the differences between their intertwined bodies.

'Sable . . . my beautiful Sable . . .' Rico released her breathless mouth to trail his lips down the soft flesh of her sunwarmed body towards the swell of her breast.

Still caught in the charm of the moment, Sable uttered a little cry of pleasure, moving spasmodically beneath him, and heard his heavy moan of response. Instinctively her hands rose to thread through the dark mass of his hair, a mischievous smile parting her lips as she recalled her responsibility for its wetness. A strange feeling was unfolding inside her, flowing through her limbs, making them heavy and lethargic, while a heavy pulse began to throb low down inside her in time with her hastened heartbeat.

Sighing, she lowered her hands, drifting them down Rico's back, feeling a wave of triumph as she felt his deep shudder. Making love with Simon had never been like this . . . Simon! She uttered a cry of distress as the warm aura of pleasure under which she'd been sheltering dissolved as if it had been exploded by a grenade.

'*Querida* . . . what is it?' Rico levered himself away from her, his eyes heavy with desire probing her face. 'Did I hurt you?'

'No.' Her voice was shaking as she sat up, reaching downward for the protection of the *pareo*, her fingers trembling so much that she was unable to tie the knot.

'Then what's wrong?' Rico's breathing was quick and ragged.

'Everything!' She forced herself to meet the stillness of his questioning eyes. 'Everything's wrong! I— we . . .' She stumbled to find the right words to excuse her actions. 'Don't you see, we were victims of our own emotions? You made me angry and I annoyed you by pushing you in the pool . . . and instead of fighting . . .' She swallowed, wishing she'd stayed by the pool and let him take his vengeance that way, instead of leaving herself open to the kind of attack she had just endured.

'We made love?' he finished her sentence. 'No, Sable. It's not as simple as that.' Reluctantly he rose to his feet in defeat, extending a hand to help her. 'What happened between us just now was no substitute for blows, and to deny the existence of any real desire between us is dishonest.'

'Dishonest!' she flared back at him, accepting his cool clasp and instantly regretting doing so as their palms met, sending a shock-wave of reaction down her bare arm. For ten days, despite her previous qualms, he hadn't laid so much as a finger on her—and then this! She met his discerning gaze with blazing condemnation. 'Don't you dare use that word to me! If anyone lacks integrity, it's you! My uncle has trusted myself and Rosina to your care, believing you to be a man of honour . . .!'

She paused to control the anger that threatened to choke her. So Rico was feeling disappointment and frustration—so what? So was she. He'd made her senses sing and her body glow, but the mock-betrothal between them gave him no rights at all to have assaulted her with such deadly expertise.

'Go on,' he invited her coldly, his jaw taut, his face

pale beneath the tan. 'You were about to comment on my honour, I believe.'

She was risking his anger, but he deserved to hear her indictment. 'Only to remind you that I'm Roberto Guimares's niece, and I expect to be treated with respect.' His stillness threatened her but she still had more to say. 'Just because you've revealed yourself as a *ranchero* rather than a *gaucho* doesn't make you any more impressive in my eyes!'

'Or any more desirable?' he enquired softly.

The question shocked her. 'I'm in love with Simon. I'm going to marry him. I don't find any other man desirable; how could I?'

Rico gave an odd laugh, completely devoid of humour. 'What has being in love got to do with physical desire?' He didn't wait for an answer from her slightly parted, panting lips, supplying it himself. 'Desire flamed between us from the first moment our eyes met, and we are both equally frustrated that we cannot claim from each other what we both want, because society denies us the right to indulge ourselves at the expense of our families' honour.'

'How dare you?' Sable fought to find the words to refute his crude assumption. 'Of course I don't want you! You forced yourself on me just now! No way did I respond!' Every fibre and cell of her body labelled her a liar as her voice cracked with desperation. Horrified and puzzled at her own weakness, she waited for Rico to denounce her. He was far too experienced not to have known the way she had met his caresses with genuine fervour.

'Here . . .' He moved towards her and with steady fingers fastened the knot of her *pareo*. 'You'd better find Rosina.' He accompanied his instruction with a little push in the direction of the club house. 'At least next time you feel like drowning me—perhaps you'll think twice!'

So it had been some kind of punishment, after all. Sable sped through the shrubbery, hearing the mocking sound of Rico's laughter behind her. What was happening to her? She should have had more pride than to allow herself to be mauled by the handsome Brazilian who had forced his way into her life. To him, it might be a joke. To her, the knowledge that she had allowed herself to enjoy those moments of sensual pleasure at his hands was shattering.

Despite the heat of the sun on her bare arms she shivered. What on earth had happened to her? She couldn't stand the sight of Rico de Braganza, and his assertion that she fancied him was ludicrous! But, nevertheless, the terrifying question she was being forced to ask herself was simple. If she hadn't suddenly thought of Simon, just how far would she have allowed Rico's caresses to go?

CHAPTER SIX

THERE was one advantage of having Latin blood in her veins, Sable opined resignedly the following day, regarding herself in the dressing-table mirror as she braided her hair before twisting it into a coronet on the top of her head—she didn't need a lot of make-up to bring her face into focus.

Unlike some of her fair-skinned English friends back home, her eyes were heavily fringed with naturally thick black lashes, the eyebrows above them equally dark but sufficiently well shaped to need only a periodic tidying up to keep their winged outline, and her full-lipped, average-sized mouth had a healthy aura of pinkness without the aid of additional colour.

Still, since tonight was Gala night at the Country Club and her whole family were going, she would gild the lily a little! Delicate fingers applied a spot of rose shader to the creamy skin of her cheekbones, a touch of ultramarine eyeshadow to enhance the deep pansy-blue of her eyes.

Satisfied that her hair was tidily in place without escaping wisps to mar the silhouette of her slim, graceful neck, she stepped into the dress she had chosen to wear. The sleeveless scarlet garment, with its deep V-neck and figure-fitting bodice above a swirling skirt of a hundred tiny pleats, had always been an eye-catcher, and tonight she wanted to look her best.

Reaching for her matching ear-rings, Sable fastened the long scarlet danglers to her neat ears, tossing her head so they swayed and tickled her neck.

78

Tonight she'd be seeing Rico again for the first time since the previous day when he'd escorted herself and Rosina back to the *hacienda*. Her cousin had been happy to chatter away inconsequentially, and had shown no sign of recognising Sable's abstinence from conversation as she exchanged pleasantries with their male companion.

Now, more than twenty-four hours later, she was still shaken by the intensity of Rico's actions. She'd never thought of herself as being weak-willed, and the fact that Rico had managed to overcome her scruples was a painful truth to live with.

Doubtless it had given him a sense of triumph to find her pliant in his arms. But to suggest he wanted to be her lover and to intimate that she desired him in the same way was scandalous! Dear heavens! How he must despise her for allowing him such liberties when she was going to marry another man. If only Simon was here with her, to hold her and tell her how much he needed her to make his life complete . . . It was his pride, of course, which had made him ask her to wait. She'd been prepared to turn her back on her father, her home and her inheritance in her eagerness to share Simon's life. But he had wanted to give her the life-style to which she'd grown accustomed . . . As if material possessions mattered when they loved each other . . . And still she had heard nothing from him. Surely the post wasn't as bad as that?

She stared at her face in the mirror, trying to compose its anguished lines. Tonight she had to face Rico again, share the evening's celebrations with him, behave as if they were sweethearts. Smile at him, talk to him and endure his touch as he held her in his arms on the dance-floor. Somehow she would manage to endure his closeness and his taunts. At least they wouldn't be alone together. In fact, she pondered, perhaps she could use the crowded ambience of the Gala to support her courage and insist their masquerade had served its purpose in protecting Rosina and the time had come to stage a lovers' quarrel and parting of the ways!

Picking up her small clutch-bag, she rose to her feet at the same moment as the door opened and Rosina popped her head round it.

'Is Uncle Roberto ready to leave?' Sable smiled at her cousin.

'Ten minutes, he said.' The younger girl advanced into the room, waving an envelope. 'I came to give you this with Papa's apologies. It was caught up in the mail left on his desk this morning.'

Simon! It had to be from Simon! All along she'd known tonight was going to be extra special. Scarcely aware of Rosina's leaving the room, Sable ripped open the envelope, her eyes devouring the beautifully written text.

Spain was great, she read. Warmer than England and the location work was progressing on schedule. He'd received her letters and was glad she was having such a good time with her Brazilian relatives. Quickly she flicked over the page, trying to find some emotion, some evidence of affection in the stilted, formal phrases.

In her own letters she'd poured out her hopes and her longings, written of her love for him, her need to be held in his arms once more—but this was no love-letter! A strange fear clamped her stomach, tightening the muscles of her diaphragm, making her breathing uneven, as she read the empty, meaningless phrases. Simon was an actor! A creative, vibrant spirit! A man who could express his thoughts with poetic eloquence . . . He couldn't have penned this trite day-to-day account . . .

Her mouth was dry as she reached the last page and her eyes read what her heart had already sensed. He'd enjoyed their friendship, he had written, and hoped she would make a success of her future. He'd had tentative approaches to go to the United States to further his own career and had the good fortune to meet a truly marvellous girl whom he was hoping to marry when shooting of the first episode was completed. He couldn't give her his new address, but he knew she would wish him well for the future—as he did her . . .

Shock lanced through her, bringing beads of sweat to her forehead. She wanted to be sick, as the implications filtered into her dazed mind, but even that relief was denied her as she sank down on the bed, her face behind its delicate make-up ashen. Her father had been right. The truth was brutally clear. Simon had never loved her. No man who had ever experienced deep feeling could have possibly written such a cold, callous note, totally denying that there had been anything but casual friendship between them. People fell out of love—that she could understand and accept, however bitter her own pain. But Simon had denied the former existence of any spark of emotion.

Suddenly she was seeing very clearly. Simon had indeed wanted her money far more than he'd wanted her. What she'd thought had been his tolerance of her refusal to anticipate their marriage had in fact been uninterest. Her money had been his goal—probably he'd been seeing other women at the same time, women who were poorer, but freer with their favours! Had her father suspected this, but spared her the ultimate humiliation of revealing it?

She shivered, hugging her own slender body, feeling the rapid beat of her heart beneath her palm. When Simon's plans to force her father into agreeing to

their marriage had been thwarted he'd lost no time in
finding a substitute, despite his vows to her. Had he just
been keeping her on ice in case she'd managed to change
her father's mind? Or had he simply lacked the courage
to tell her face to face that without her father's approval
she had nothing to offer him? She had lost her father's
love, his respect, even his interest in her future well-
being, for a cause that had been rotten to the core.
Jaime Guimares had warned her and she had flung his
warning and his paternal affection straight back in his
face . . .

'Sable—are you coming?' Rosina's light call broke
into her bitter analysis, as Sable lifted empty eyes to
meet her own ghost-like reflection in the mirror. Words
and phrases she'd written to Simon came back to haunt
her, making her cringe. She'd bared her heart to him
and he'd humiliated her beyond anything she'd ever
dreamed of. If he hadn't been embarrassed by her flow
of letters and wanted to put a stop to them, the
probability was she would never have heard from him
again.

Every instinct prompted her to make some excuse to
stay at the *hacienda*, but what could she say? Pride
fought her misery. She was a performer, wasn't she?
She might have lost everything in life she cared for, but
she would prove her mettle. Tonight she'd give the
performance of her life.

'Yes, I'm ready.' Too stunned to weep, she walked
stiffly towards the door.

Lights, laughter, music . . . The grounds of the Club
were alive with sound and movement. Alone at Roberto
Guimares's table, Sable stared unseeingly at the glass in
her hand. Somewhere among the crowds Luis and
Toninho were pursuing their own pleasures, while

Rosina, having plucked up courage to introduce Aleixo, present as a guest, to her father, had taken the former on to the specially laid outside dance-floor.

She herself had accepted an invitation to dance from a young man at a neighbouring table, and in her temporary absence her uncle and aunt had disappeared in the crowd.

Automatically she raised the glass to her lips, scarcely aware of the potent spirit which burned down her throat, too numb to feel anything other than an appalling sense of loss.

What was wrong with her, that she lacked the power to make people love her? First there had been her mother—deserting her when she'd been a mere toddler—leaving her in the efficient but impersonal care of her father.

Then, when she'd dared to oppose his unilateral and unfair plans to force an arranged marriage on her, not only had he accepted without query that she'd betrayed her moral upbringing, but, having arranged for her to be taken out of his sight, he hadn't even cared enough to get in touch to find out how she was, or left an address where he could be contacted in an emergency. Jaime Guimares had washed his hands of his errant daughter, and it would have served him right, she thought with a sudden spurt of energy, if she *had* formed an unwelcome alliance in Brazil and gone ahead with marriage plans to underline her independence!

She took another long swallow of her drink, discerning the taste of rum and lemon in the heady cocktail she'd ordered herself from the bar, her thoughts continuing their trend. Now there was Simon, on whom she'd pinned all her faith. Handsome, talented Simon, whose blond good looks had been such a perfect foil to her own darkness. Simon too had joined the ranks of those disowning Sable Guimares . . . and finally there was Rico de Braganza, who had faithfully promised to meet her at the Club and who hadn't bothered to grace the proceedings with his arrogant presence! She clenched her teeth, refusing to let the weight of disillusionment she was suffering crush her.

'Our dance, I believe . . .' At the sound of his familiar voice so close to her ear Sable gave a startled cry, turning in her chair to gaze up at him, her breath catching in her throat as she met his dark, steady gaze.

Dressed in a light jacket over dark trousers, his pale shirt gleaming in the subdued light, Rico looked magnificent, but Sable was in no mood to be impressed.

'I'm not dancing,' she said coldly. 'But since you've decided to put in an appearance, you can get me another drink from the bar.' She pushed her empty glass towards him.

Studiously he ignored both her imperious order and her gesture, pulling out a chair beside her and seating himself.

'I'm sorry I couldn't be here to meet you. I was delayed on important business,' he said quietly, his dark eyes travelling slowly over her strained face and rigidly held body. 'I hadn't realised that my not being here to greet you would have distressed you so deeply.'

'Oh, don't apologise!' she laughed brittly. 'No one is more used to business interfering with pleasure than I am.'

She should have stopped there, but suddenly her tongue was running away with her as the pent-up hurt of years came tumbling out. 'You remind me of my father. Do you know that all the time I was away at school he never came to see me once? Oh, he was very generous financially—the best school, all the extras: horse-riding, ski-ing, private music lessons—but I'd have sacrificed them all to have him present at just one of the speech-days, or on my birthday, but there was always something happening to keep him away!' It was impossible to hide the bitterness in her tone, remembering the silent tears she'd shed on so many occasions when she'd seen her schoolfriends' families depart from a prize-giving hugging and kissing their excited offspring.

'But according to what you've told me, not only did he have a business to run,' Rico riposted gently, 'but he lacked a wife to give him the love and support a man needs when times are tough. I guess he showed his love by working for you, so you could reap the benefits of his labour . . .'

'But he never cared for what I really wanted!' she challenged the man beside her, her pale face becoming animated with passion, as she gave full rein to her self-pity. 'When he agreed to my going to drama college I was overjoyed, but he never intended me to become a cabaret artiste like my mother—which was my ambition. He was just playing for time, waiting until I was "mature" enough to be married off to some elderly Brazilian friend of his. A widower, a man I'd never met, and of whose existence I'd never been told!'

There! Under her present stress the shameful admission had slipped out, as she recognised out loud that to her father she'd been nothing more than an acquisition to be traded in his own interests.

'Sable, *meu amor* . . .' Rico's firm-fingered, beautifully manicured hand with its toughened palm closed compassionately over her own as it rested on the table, his face serious with concern at her outburst. 'What is it? What's happened?'

Desperately she fought to bring her tremulous voice

under control, unwilling to make a public scene. God knew how much she'd needed to talk to someone about the way her father had betrayed her, how he'd planned to parcel her up and send her away to some boyhood companion without a thought for her emotional fulfilment.

She must be mad to select Rico as the recipient of her pent-up miseries, but who else was there? Raising her gaze to his quiet face, she read encouragement to continue in the depths of his dark eyes. At least he wasn't attempting to shut her up, as some men would have done, she acknowledged shakily. Neither was he lecturing her, she realised with surprised relief.

'I—I wanted to have someone of my own, someone close to me I could . . .' She wanted to say 'love' but the word stuck in her throat. 'Someone I could care for,' she compromised. 'And then I met Simon . . .'

Dear lord, what was she doing? She'd never meant to tell anyone what she'd just learned of Simon's perfidy. Tears choked in her throat. If only she'd been given more time to get used to what had happened, instead of having had to leave the house directly . . . Perhaps she wasn't such a good actress as she'd hoped. Angrily she brushed her free hand across her eyes.

'Go on, Sable.' Darkly intense, Rico's eyes imprisoned her own as his hand tightened against hers, firm reassuring fingers promising her his unmitigated attention. 'What about Simon?'

Her turbulent emotions were too strong for her mental reservations as she responded to Rico's sympathetic aura, spilling out her agony without reservation. 'When I met Simon it was as if my prayers had been answered. I thought the two of us . . .' Suppressed tears made her voice tremble. 'But it's all over. I got the news just before we left the *hacienda* to come here. Simon's gone, left me, found another girl to marry.'

By some miracle she'd got her tears under control, managing to conjure up a falsely bright smile to turn on the still face of the man beside her. 'So you see, my father spoiled that dream, too . . .'

'He saved you from a nightmare!' The power of Rico's response stunned her, as his dark gaze searched the paleness of her face. 'Can't you see, he must have known what the man was like. He didn't want to see you hurt!'

'And I'm not now?' Her passionate face defied him to deny her agony. 'Do you think I worried about sharing my inheritance with Simon?' There was pride as well as pain in the depth of her sparkling eyes. 'I would have given him everything I had,' she declared fiercely. 'And we would have been happy if Papa hadn't interfered!'

'You would have been miserable, *minha* Sable,' his harsh voice corrected her. 'Because in any relationship of love one has to give as well as take, and the man who took your father's bribe would have taken everything from you and given nothing in return.'

'No!' she defended heatedly, rising to her feet. 'In any case, I don't want to discuss it any more. After all this is supposed to be a Gala night. Why don't we dance?' Falsely bright, she flashed him a brilliant smile.

Silently Rico rose to his feet, holding out his arm to her, leading her on to the floor, supporting and guiding her light weight as she surrendered herself to his arms.

How solid and comforting his strong masculine frame felt, how resolute the power of his arms . . . When he pulled her even closer into his embrace Sable made no attempt to oppose him. When he lowered his head to rest his cheek against her own unnaturally warm skin she revelled in his nearness, her senses appreciating the tangy scent of cologne and the warm, masculine fragrance of him that was as heady as the flickering lights around them and the pulsating beat of the samba band. Closing her eyes, she relaxed against him, allowing him to take her where he would, while the long-suppressed tears trickled down her face.

It was only when the music stopped, and a short musicians' break was announced and she was faced with returning to Roberto Guimares's table to confront the whole family, that Sable's courage finally deserted her.

'Rico, I can't let them see me yet, not like this,' she protested weakly, gratefully accepting the spotless white handkerchief he offered her to mop her damp cheeks.

'Do you want to go back to the *hacienda*?' he asked quietly. 'I can easily tell them you've got a headache.'

'Please.' She nodded her dark head, standing back in the shadow as he made his leisurely way across the floor.

Minutes later she was settling down thankfully against the soft upholstery of a white Mercedes and closing her eyes as Rico turned it in the direction of Roberto's home.

'I'm sorry I interrupted your evening,' she apologised stiffly as the maid who'd opened the door for them retreated. 'It was very good of you to drive me back. I hope I haven't ruined the night for you.'

'I only went there to see you,' he averred uncompromisingly, shutting the front door quietly behind him. 'We have to talk, Sable—you and I.'

'Yes, I know,' she agreed wearily, recalling her earlier decision to announce the parting of their ways. 'But does it have to be now?'

'I believe so, yes.' He walked towards the main *salon*, opening the door and indicating she precede him into the room. Placing gentle hands on her shoulders, he commanded her attention as she turned towards him. She could fee the dry warmth of his palms as he fixed her wide blue eyes with an intent scrutiny.

'Sable—this pretence between us has continued long enough.' He paused momentarily, his voice deepening. 'I want you to marry me.' Ignoring her gasp of shocked dissension, he took her into his arms, pulling her against his lean hard length. Instantly she felt a thrill of expectation run through her body, a pang of something she could only identify as the beginning of desire.

'Marry you?' she gasped in disbelief. 'That's ridiculous! We don't even like each other.'

He smiled, a charming twist of his lips. ' "Like" is too tepid a word to describe what exists between us, *meu amor*. There is nothing ridiculous in my desiring you, though some might consider me rash in offering you the status of my wife after such a short acquaintance, but it's time that Ribatejo had a mistress and I a wife to warm my bed and bear my children, and you are a beautiful and passionate woman—Isabella Guimares. You will suit me very well, I think and now the obstacle of your unsatisfactory lover has been resolved, what is there to prevent it?'

'Me!' Sable's voice trembled with shock as she recognised that between herself and this audacious philanderer who had turned her confidences against her there existed a basic chemistry which could defeat all her good intentions to deny him, and he had chosen this, her weakest moment, to sway her. 'I can prevent it! I . . . I . . .' She had been going to say she hated him, detested him with all the power at her disposal, but the words had frozen on her tongue, as some inner sense prompted her to re-analyse her emotions. Certainly she was experiencing some very powerful feeling for Rico de Braganza as he stood there uttering his impertinent proposal and gazing down into her eyes with all the force of his strong personality—but hate? No, definitely not that.

'Sable . . .' He breathed her name, raising his hand, allowing his thumb to caress the soft skin of her cheek, drawing it down to follow the delicate line of her jaw before tracing the outline of her parted lips. 'Don't tell me you don't feel this attraction between us. Yesterday, when I found you in the clearing and you returned my caresses with such passion, I knew you were mine to take when the time and place was right.'

At that moment she couldn't have told him anything if her life had depended on it. Too disturbed and excited by his words and his proximity for argument, she made an effort to escape his commanding hold, but it was to no avail as his hands slid down her body, following its slender curves, moulding her tightly against his own aroused form, telling her without words the extent of his desire.

'Rico . . .' She gasped his name. He was trading on her confessed need to be loved, but not like this! She wanted soft words and endearments, compliments about her personality and appearance, protestations of never-ending love like Simon had given to her. Simon! The irony struck her immediately. She was saying she would prefer a litany of lies rather than the honest declaration that Rico's virile body impressed upon her!

'Rico—please!'

He must have misunderstood her plea for release, because instead of freeing her he swept her up into his arms, carrying her towards one of the long leather chesterfield couches, depositing her boneless body on its softness and following her down. One hand sought her throat, moving smooth fingers along its length, positioning her head so he could lower his own and discover the dark warmth of her mouth. His kiss was urgent, his mouth hungry and exacting as it sought possession, lips warm and sensuous, arrogantly demanding a passionate response to meet their own attack.

Beneath his onslaught Sable was defenceless, her mind spinning helplessly, her body quivering abjectly as the warm flood of desire Rico had first aroused in her the previous day swelled to a floodtide in his embrace. Was it possible to resent and desire a man at the same time?

Rico's mouth was still commanding her own when he raised his hands to her head, unfastening the pins that secured her hair, drawing down its ebony wealth to fall against the delicate skin of her shoulders. Eyes so dark they could have been black glittered with a hungry intent in his lean face, sending shock-waves of apprehesion through every inch of her body.

'Marry me, Sable. Be my wife . . .' His breathing was heavy, his voice rasping as he pushed the wide neckline of her dress past one shoulder, sliding his fingers inside to find and capture the taut, swelling curve of her breast. 'Give me the right to enjoy you—all of you . . .'

'I can't marry you—I don't love you!' she protested desperately.

'Are you such an infallible judge of what love is, hmm?' he taunted her softly.

No, she wasn't, she agreed silently. Once she had thought both Simon and her father had loved her. Now, to her bitter regret, she knew she had been living in cloud-cuckoo land. But surely it wasn't possible that the fiery antagonism that flared between her and Rico at the slightest provocation had its roots in anything but mutual aversion? Though if so, why could his touch set her alight?

'But we hardly know each other—and we quarrel all the time . . .' she said weakly.

'Not all the time,' he corrected gently, and she was forced to remember almost against her will the moments of calm and shared pleasures they had enjoyed together in the previous days. 'And when we did it was only because the image of Simon stood between us as an aggravation.'

Ignoring her soft moan of denial, he continued softly, 'And as for hardly knowing each other, there will be time enough for that in the years ahead.'

'No . . . no . . .' But the protest was half-hearted, her dark head rolling in torment against the cream leather beneath it as his fingers touched the sensitised peak of the tender flesh beneath them. Ignoring her agonised response, Rico made a small sound somewhere between a groan and gasp, as he lowered his own head and with infinite finesse kissed the hardened apex his hand had nurtured.

Beneath the intimate caress Sable stiffened and arched, her body crying out for release even as her heart and mind strove to understand the turbulent emotions that threatened their stability. Urgent hands seeking to disrobe her further gave her the incentive for further objection.

'Rico—no more—I beg you——' She grasped the hand that would have found and lowered the zip fastening at the back of her dress.

His hand stilled in her hold. 'Because you don't like it? Or because you believe such joy is best reserved for when we are married, *querida*?'

'Both—neither——' Her heart was beating fast as she sought logical objections to persuade herself as much as the forceful Brazilian who was weaving such a powerful spell over her responses. 'Marriage between us is unthinkable. For one thing, my father would oppose us.' But in some secret part of her mind she *was* thinking about it, held in the grip of a fierce excitement.

'But it's only *your* agreement I need, *minha* Sable.' His voice was hoarse as his dark eyes devoured her, willing her to cede to him. 'I have no need for your father's approval or your fortune. I have ample means to provide for you and the family we shall raise together.'

She hesitated, too confused and disturbed by the events of the past few hours to trust her own reactions. What would it be like to live on Rico's vast ranch, to organise his home, to lie in his arms at night and to experience the full explosive power of his possession, to bear his children? Might there not be more satisfaction to that than trying to follow a stage career in direct opposition to Jaime Guimares's wishes when she returned to England?

At least she could be sure Rico de Braganza was no fortune-hunter, and his need for her was honest and intense enough to offer her marriage for the privilege of enjoying her body. The truth was that marriage to him would free her for ever from her father's domination and wipe out the humiliation she had suffered at his and Simon's hands.

A surge of bitterness flooded through her veins. She had been deserted by both the man who'd sworn he loved her, and her father. As for her own feelings, she might not ever be able to love another man after Simon's deception, but Rico was magnificently attractive, and it was true her body had responded to him with an eagerness that had shocked her. Certainly they were physically compatible . . . Could that possibly be a firm enough foundation on which to base a marriage?

She shivered in a dreadful anticipation, suddenly terrifyingly aware that she found something very attractive in what she was being offered, but hovering on the brink of confessing as much to Rico, so outrageous and inexplicable did the admission strike her.

'Sable . . .?' It was a mere whisper, intended not to break the spell as his brilliant eyes read and translated the passage of her thoughts. 'Don't you see it was Fate that brought us together?'

She shuddered. He sounded so determined, so sure of himself. Only one table lamp illuminated the large room, and in its limited light his form assumed giant proportions as he rose lazily to his feet to stand staring down at her. Gazing at the hard lines of his face, the easy power of his long-legged stance, she was almost persuaded that their meeting had been forecast in their stars, and she had no real power to oppose it . . .

'Rico . . . I . . .' She paused to gather her senses together before irrevocably committing herself.

The next moment she was drawing in an anguished breath of utter horror as the closed door to the room was thrust open and Renata Guimares appeared on the threshold.

'My dear, Rico told us you had a headache and were coming home, but Rosina said you'd received a letter from Europe and that something in it might have upset you. I . . .'

Having advanced into the room, after switching on the powerful chandelier suspended from the centre of the ceiling, she stopped in confusion, the colour rising to her cheeks as Sable grasped the lowered top of her dress, dragging it up to cover her naked skin and Rico moved to shield her body from her aunt's embarrassed gaze.

Decent again, but with nothing able to disguise her tousled hair and love-swollen lips, Sable watched in dismay as Roberto Guimares followed his wife into the room. The scale, so delicately balanced, had received a stunning impact she couldn't ignore. She saw his face darken, and before he could speak one word of defamation she was on her feet, taking her place beside Rico, resting her hand on the light fabric which covered his arm.

'Uncle Roberto, Aunt Renata . . . Rico and I want you to be the first to know. We've decided that since Papa is not available for prior consultation, we're going ahead with our wedding without his blessing, at the earliest possible date.'

CHAPTER SEVEN

'YOU'RE the most glamorous bride I've ever seen!' Rosina peeked at herself over Sable's shoulder, smoothing down the rose-pink satin of her own simply styled dress. 'Who could possibly have guessed my wanting to elope with Aleixo could have led to this?'

'Who, indeed?' Sable shot her cousin an affectionate smile as she stared at her own reflection, pinning a spray of white gardenias into her hair to mask the clips that held her light veil in place.

She'd fully anticipated a quiet wedding without the involvement of her new-found family, but her uncle and aunt had been adamant. In her father's absence they were her next of kin, and it was their utmost pleasure to give her the kind of ceremony and send-off he would have wanted.

'It's not as if you're making an ill-advised union,' Roberto Guimares had told her gently. 'Rico de Braganza is a wealthy man, whose business reputation is flawless. As his wife you will have everything a girl could wish for—a fine residence, an enviable social position . . .'

Sable had nodded demurely, thinking how similar her uncle's priorities were to her father's. Whatever her reasons for agreeing to become Rico's bride, they didn't include his wealth or background, that at least she was sure of!

She turned from the mirror in a flurry of white lace skirts and headed for the window. Outside she could see the full panoply of the wedding reception to come. Long trestle tables covered in white linen, already prepared to receive the vast amount of food that outside caterers would be providing and putting into place while the marriage was being celebrated in the local church; individual tables scattered around the large paved area, each one bedecked with flowers beneath bright sunshades to protect the guests from the power of the afternoon sun.

Did Rico love her? It was the question never far from her thoughts . . . She stared down at her left hand where a ring of twisted diamonds and emeralds glittered against her flawless skin, and felt the proverbial butterflies fluttering in her stomach. Did he? He'd spoken to her about his need for a wife, his wish to settle down and raise a family, but he'd never actually told her he loved her. Wanted her—yes, and the passion and power of his smoothly muscled body had confirmed his verbal attestation. But surely the fact that he had proposed marriage rather than attempting to seduce her without any promises proved that she had some value to him rather than just the physical?

She'd known him for such a short time, and he'd pressurised her to make a decision when all her previous hopes had just crumbled at her feet. Her body had thrilled to his touch, and the wanton excitement she'd always felt in his presence was undeniable, although she'd only come to realise how potent that was in the last few days . . . Certainly her own motives in accepting his unexpected proposal had been mixed: a heady amalgam of physical longing allied to a need for revenge against both her father and Simon Layton, brought to an emotive climax at the sight of her aunt's stunned expression.

Yet during the past week she had suffered no regrets, only a mounting excitement at the prospect before her.

Was it possible that she was beginning to fall in love with Rico, she wondered bemusedly, or had she merely allowed herself to be swept away by the sheer dominance of his attractive persona when she was at her lowest ebb?

She sighed, aware that she needed more time before she could answer that question. She still knew so little about him—but she was learning all the time. Her first surprise had been when he'd told her he would be issuing no invitations to the wedding on his own behalf, other than to Aleixo, shrugging away her questioning look with nonchalant ease. 'My only close relations are an uncle and aunt who are holidaying in the US at the moment, and a cousin whose wife is expecting their second child at any day. Obviously she can't make the journey from São Paulo, and Vitor would never leave her.'

'Is anything wrong, Sable?' Rosina's light voice penetrated her thoughts. 'You're not having second thoughts, are you . . .'

'No, of course not!' She turned an affectionate glance to the younger girl. Even if she had entertained doubts, at this stage there was no honourable way out. And she didn't really want one, did she? Her major regret was that she hadn't seen much of Rico since her dramatic decision, as he'd been absent from the *hacienda* most of the time, finalising the investigation at the Granja Branca, before their departure on honeymoon to Rio de Janeiro.

So they'd met briefly, mostly in the company of others, and their conversation had been limited to the hundred and one arrangements necessary to send them off in the style Roberto Guimares had insisted they deserved. Of course, her father would reimburse her uncle for the expense when he found out about it.

Whether or not he approved, he would hardly allow his brother to shoulder the entire cost, although Roberto had declared himself proud and honoured to do so.

Anger burgeoned inside her as she moved away from the window. It wasn't the first time that Jaime Guimares had put himself out of touch. His habit of jetting around the world often made it impossible to reach him, and this time had been no exception. Despite Roberto's efforts to make contact, he had consistently failed. For a brief moment a mist of tears blinded Sable's eyes before she blinked them clear. Why should she care, anyway? He would probably have disapproved of both Rico and her defiant acceptance of his proposal, and done his utmost to prevent the ceremony taking place!

'Rosina, my dear, are you with Sable?' Roberto's voice outside the bedroom door claimed their joint attention. 'It's about time you were leaving with your mother and Toninho.'

As Rosina opened the door to obey her father, Roberto Guimares stepped across the threshold and advanced into the room. 'Sable, my dear . . .' His voice was gruff, his eyes moist. 'What can I possibly say to you? You look magnificent! My only regret is that your father can't be here today to see you like this. It would be the proudest day of his life!'

'Oh, surely not, Uncle?' It was an effort to keep her voice light but she managed it. 'Surely that will come when he successfully completes the business deal that's keeping him incommunicado?'

'Don't judge him too harshly, *menina*.' Sadness lengthened Roberto's face. 'He could hardly have foreseen this happening.'

'Business always was very important to Papa.' She managed to twist her lips into a smile. There was no point in distressing Uncle Roberto by letting him know how much she doubted whether knowledge of her impending nuptials would have dragged Jaime Guimares away from his takeover, unless it had been to abort the proceedings! Proud? She cringed inwardly at her secret knowledge. Jaime Guimares had long since stopped being proud of his errant daughter!

He hadn't even troubled to speak to her on the phone all the time she'd been there—that was the extent of his indifference! And there'd been no reply from the London house when she'd tried to contact him there. Recalling his intent to close the premises down, she'd been more frustrated than surprised. When Roberto's enquiries had failed, she'd tried desperately to track him down at one of his clubs, but had drawn a blank. There was a limit to the number of expensive phone calls she could made across the Atlantic at her relatives' expense, so in the end she'd reluctantly abandoned her enquiries. It just felt so wrong, though: walking out of his life without giving him the opportunity of a last filial embrace, however unlikely the possibility he would take it!

'Are you ready to leave, *menina*?' Roberto's gruff voice pierced her thoughts. 'Or do you mean to keep your bridegroom waiting your pleasure?'

Giving herself one cursory glance in the mirror, dispassionately surveying the picture she made, hair upswept to form a raven crown beneath the flimsy veil with its embellishment of gardenias, face made up with the delicacy of skills well learned, Sable assured herself that the wardrobe and make-up were perfect, the props supplied by her family were first class and the leading man . . .

Briefly, out of curiosity, she tried to conjure up Simon's image, but the screen of her mind betrayed her, reminding her instead of the hard, lean face of Rico de Braganza, the lustrous eyes and the sensual mouth that had dared to touch her own within an hour of their first meeting. He had been a stranger then and he remained a stranger now. Tonight all that would change. Tonight they would join in the most intimate of all human relationships and a new phase of her life would begin.

'I'm quite ready, Uncle,' she told him calmly. The serene mask of her role firmly fixed in place, Sable walked gracefully towards the older man and took his arm.

'This one's mine!' It was six hours later when Toninho approached Sable from behind, curling his arm round her waist and spinning her into his arms as the samba band stirred up the rhythm of the dance.

'Why not?' she agreed with a laugh, allowing herself to be swept into the crowd of happy couples enjoying themselves at her uncle's expense. Her veil discarded in her bedroom, the gardenias consigned to the vase by her bed, Sable was riding on a high wave of exultation, composed of nervous tension, a reckless disregard for the immediate future and a possible surfeit of *cachaça* if she were to be honest with herself.

Her body, still clothed in the white lace of her newly consecrated state, moved effortlessly, following her cousin's lead, her feet moving to the rhythm, as her mind strayed back to the service.

The small church had been overflowing. Rico's lack of family supporters more than compensated by the friends and neighbours of the Guimares. Roberto was a well-known and respected personage. He entertained widely and was well-liked—and what South American could resist the excitement of a wedding and all the following celebrations?—certainly not a Brazilian whose life was filled with the annual joy of carnival!

Somehow she'd expected Rico to treat the ceremony lightly, but there'd been nothing insouciant about the man who had turned to watch her walk up the aisle. Immaculately dressed in a dark drey suit with a lighter grey waistcoat, a silver tie knotted at his throat and a white carnation in his buttonhole, Ricardo de Braganza had looked every inch the wealthy landowner he claimed to be. Was she the only person in that whole crowded building that knew the soul of a privateer lurked beneath that flawless exterior?

Ultimately, she had to admit, it was Rico who had played his part the better, repeating his vows in a clear, steady voice, gazing into her eyes with a quiet triumph that she found impressive, while she herself stumbled through the responses.

Walking through the congregation afterwards, his heavy gold ring a distracting sensation on her slim finger, she'd been glad of the support of his strong arm round her waist, although the proximity of his body disturbed her. No longer did she have the right to order him from her side. She could of course request it, but in a ceremony lasting forty-five minutes the right to enforce it had been taken from her—a prospect she was beginning to find daunting.

'Oh!' For a second her concentration wavered and she missed the rhythm. 'I'm sorry, Toninho—did I step on your foot?'

'If you did, it felt less than a butterfly alighting.' He grinned at her, a good-looking young man a few months older than herself, seldom at a loss for words. 'But don't you think you ought to give it a rest now? I don't believe you've stopped since the music began. I don't want your bridegroom taking me to task.'

There was an edge of wariness in his voice that

amazed her.

'You're not serious, Toninho?' Raised eyebrows begged him to confirm it. 'Rico's not my keeper, and even if he were he could hardly object to my dancing with my cousin!'

'You've got a lot to learn about us, I'm afraid, Sable.' His voice was serious, his smooth brow wrinkled with intensity. 'Brazilian men take their masculinity very seriously still. Whatever may have happened in the north of this continent, here it remains a patriarchal society.'

'So?' She raised innocent eyes to his countenance.

Toninho sighed. 'So—you'd do well to remember it. In Brazil it's not enough for a man to be male—he has to prove his virility to anyone who casts a doubt on it. And that, dear cousin, means that men are possessive of everything that is their own—and even more possessive of their wives and girlfriends!'

'But . . .' Sable began combing her fingers through her hair, dislodging one of the clips holding it in place. 'But that's an antediluvian attitude . . .'

'Perhaps.' Toninho shrugged, his shoulders leaving her with the impression that even this minor concession to her opinion was out of politeness rather than conviction. 'But one which it's in your own interests to remember. Look, Sable . . .' He lowered his voice confidentially as he led her away from the throng on the dance-floor. 'What I'm trying to say is—it might be better if you introduce him slowly to the liberated side of your character,' he finished abruptly.

'Thank you.' Sable bowed her head to hide the gleam of amusement in her eyes, deciding that Rico would have to take her as he found her but refraining from shocking her cousin by opining this aloud. 'You're very sweet, Toninho. I really have enjoyed the weeks we've spent together. Is there anything else I should know about Brazilian customs?'

'Just one more.' He fumbled in his trouser pocket and brought forth a small box. 'There's one thing you can't buy for yourself and I thought you should have.' He gave her a wry smile laced with affection. 'You're making a very big change in the life you used to lead—I think you may need it!'

Wonderingly she took the gift, opening the lid to gaze down at a small charm, obviously made of gold and fashioned in the form of a clenched fist with the thumb sticking up between the first and second finger. Carefully she lifted it and found it was attached to a fine gold chain.

'Why, Toninho, it's beautiful!' she exclaimed.

'It's a *figa*.' He was delighted at her obvious pleasure. 'It has magical powers that will ward off evil from you—but for it to be effective you cannot buy one for yourself—it must be a gift.'

'Oh, Toninho . . .' Sable felt a lump rise in her throat. Impulsively she leaned towards him and planted a soft kiss on his cheek. 'It's lovely. Every time I wear it I'll think of you!'

'I'm glad you like it.' A faint hint of pink tingeing his suntanned face, as if he was embarrassed by her show of emotion, he turned away, leaving her clasping the small charm in the palm of her hand. Carefully she replaced it in its nest of cotton wool. Dear heavens, but she was hot! The fairy lights strung round the patio had been on for over an hour, but the evening still retained the heat of the day.

Besides, she admitted honestly, she'd managed to down an inordinate quantity of *cachaça* in between the long dances she'd been expending her nervous energy on, Uncle Roberto having pounced on Rico immediately after their arrival back at the *hacienda* to take him around introducing him to their eagerly curious guests. She put the back of her hand to her forehead, testing its heat, at the same time feeling a long tendril of hair tickle her neck. She must look a wreck!

Glancing around, she saw the party was well under way, increasing in noise and activity all the time. She just had to put the charm away safely and redress her hair. No one would miss her if she sneaked away for half an hour.

In the sanctuary of her bedroom she put Toninho's gift away in her small jewellery box before unpinning her hair completely and reaching for a brush to smooth its raven silk into a shroud of darkness round her shoulders. Oh, what a relief! And how much more comfortable she'd feel if she could get out of this wretched dress.

She half turned to the mirror, eyeing the tiny buttons that fastened the fitted dress into place and which ran from her neck to below her waist. No chance! Not with the tightly fitted sleeves that followed so faithfully the slender line of her arm to the waist and prevented any lateral movement.

'So this is where you've taken refuge, *meu amor*.'

'Oh!' Sable jumped at the unexpected interruption to her thoughts as Rico's drawl broke the silence of the room. Outside, the incessant rhythm of the samba band provided a constant background of noise, but inside she heard only Rico's steady breathing, as with a lazy hand he removed the glass from her fingers, passing it thoughtfully just beneath the flaring nostrils of his elegant nose.

'It's lemonade!' Sable informed him tightly, bristling at the implied criticism she could read on his frowning face.

'So it is,' he agreed equably, taking a deep sip to
empty the glass before placing it on the dressing-table
top before her. 'And very refreshing too, after all your
exertion.'

'Is something troubling you?' Her pulse quickened in
her throat as, sensitive to his mood, she felt the prickle
of tension in the atmosphere.

Rico's eyes narrowed fractionally. 'As the only man
present who has not had the pleasure of dancing with
you, am I not entitled to seek you out and discover why
you've been avoiding me, *querida*?'

Astonished by his harsh attitude, Sable shot him a
startled look. 'Whatever gave you that idea?'

'Ah, then I was mistaken?' There was an odd quality
in his smile which had Sable suppressing an
overwhelming urge to return to the reception. He was
too close, she thought frantically, feeling the scrutiny of
his dark eyes burning through the delicate fabric of her
wedding dress. She needed time to get used to the fact
that they were husband and wife. 'Yet it appears to me
that my presence here now is not entirely welcome?'

He had read her thoughts too clearly. 'You must
forgive me, Rico.' She said unsteadily. 'I'm afraid I
found the ceremony rather a strain.'

'As I did too.' The unexpected admission surprised
her.

'I thought it was what you wanted . . .'

Inside she was trembling, feeling once more that
inexplicable magnetism that drew her towards him, that
terrible awareness that made the small hairs on her neck
bristle. Like a charge of static electricity it pricked at her
nerves. Rico de Braganza was a dangerous man, she was
sure of it. More so than ever now he had legal authority
over her.

His sultry glance ranged over her taut body. 'Indeed it

was, *meu amor*.'

Mesmerised by the brilliance of his gaze, she swallowed, as he moved closer to her. He smelt delicious. It was a scent she couldn't put a name to, not woody or spicy but somehow a mixture of both, with a lemony tang that aroused a deep longing to open her lips and discover for herself if he tasted as beautiful as he smelled.

'Fortunately your apparent neglect of me is easily remedied . . .'

Without waiting for her reaction, he drew her into his embrace, his mouth homing in on her parted lips. Suddenly she was moving her own hands downwards, sliding them beneath his jacket, feeling her way beneath the formal waistcoat and trembling as they encountered the heat of his body beneath the white wedding shirt.

It was no brutal intrusion, no fearful violent invasion, no triumphant declaration of ownership, as she had half anticipated. Rico's first kiss as her husband was gentle and sensual and terrifyingly potent, and Sable felt her whole body respond to it, a warm spiral of excitement unfolding deep inside her, making her limbs tingle as her breasts hardened painfully against his strong chest.

Then it was over. Slowly he released her, holding her shivering body away from him, as she fought to regain the control of her senses. Now she was sure! Rico did love her! No man could kiss a woman so passionately yet so generously unless his heart as well as his body was involved!

'I think perhaps we should rejoin our guests, hmm? You look a little flushed, *meu amor*,' he mused lazily, his eyes mercilessly fixed to her warm cheeks, 'especially, since your drink is now finished, you'll have to go back to the party to obtain another one. Unless . . .' he paused meaningfully, his dark Latin eyes raking the soft outlines of her body, giving her the feeling he could sense its agitation beneath the virginal lace which clothed it '. . . unless you would prefer me to obtain refreshment for you and bring it back here?'

'No!' she said too quickly. 'I mean—no, thank you. I'd like to get some fresh air.' However innocent the suggestion, all she wanted was to get away from him and mingle with the excited crowd outside, and there'd been something about the gleam in Rico's eyes that had hinted it hadn't been innocent at all, and this was neither the time nor the place to carry their lovemaking to its logical conclusion! Not while her senses were still befuddled by the alcohol she'd sipped and while they could be interrupted at any moment by a member of her family.

Besides, in an hour or so they would be leaving the *hacienda* for a luxury hotel in the city of Porto Alegre for the first night of their married life, before boarding the early afternoon flight to Rio the next day. Alone together, with the long night stretching ahead of them, they would be able to discover each other leisurely, with passion and pleasure.

Shivering at her own wanton thoughts, Sable moved towards the door as the extension telephone beside her bed beeped. It was Rico, standing nearest to it, who raised the receiver to his ear, the sudden tautness of his jaw relaxing as, after instructing a connection to be made, he listened in silence for a few seconds before his mouth widened in a grin of utter delight.

'That's fantastic news, Vitor! And Ria—she's all right?' His eyes sparkled darkly. 'It's a day for a double celebration, then! Yes, yes, she's with me now.' He glanced across the space separating them to include Sable in his reference, then nodded. 'Of course, I should be honoured . . .' There was a slight pause as Sable returned his gaze expectantly, then his voice took on a special warmth. 'Many congratulations, Ria . . . yes, of course we understood, although Vitor has no cause for complaint. I recall I wasn't even invited to your wedding . . .' He gave a deep growl of laughter. 'I know you didn't . . .'

A tap at the half-open door distracted Sable's attention for a moment, and drawing it open she found herself gazing on Rosina's excited face. 'Papa's been looking for Rico, he particularly wants him to meet an old friend of his.' She paused seeing Rico standing there, phone in hand. 'Shall I tell him you're too busy?'

'No.' He masked the receiver with one hand. 'I'll be right there.' Turning to Sable, he held out the telephone. 'It's my cousin's wife—Ria Fortunato. She gave birth to a daughter a few hours ago, and particularly wants to have a word with you.'

'Ria? It's Sable.' She accepted the receiver, delighted at the other girl's news. She hadn't had to meet Vitor or his wife to be prepared to like them, since it was clear an extremely strong bond of kinship existed between Rico and his cousins. 'Congratulations on your news. You must be thrilled!'

'Delirious!' The pleasant, light voice the other end of the line was bubbling with joy. 'I did wonder if Vitor would have preferred another son, but he's thrilled with Caterina. I'm just sorry she chose such an inconvenient time to arrive. We're both sad that we had to miss your wedding. Ricardo's just agreed to be godfather, so we're hoping that when you come over for the christening you'll be able to stay a week or so with us.' Her voice grew a little wistful. 'Did Ricardo tell you my father was English?' She didn't wait for an answer. 'Unfortunately he died before I was born, but I have a grandfather over there and we visited him last year. I'd love to be able to talk to you about it.'

'I'd enjoy that too, Ria,' Sable responded sincerely. 'I can't wait to see your family.'

The other girl laughed. 'Nor I to see you, Sable! You know, I feel I know you quite well already. Ricardo was always so proud of you. He carried your photograph everywhere. I remember he was quite amazed when I told him he oughtn't to take your agreement to your father's suggestion for granted.' She sighed. 'But I dare say you realise what the men in this family are like. When they set their mind on anything, they don't rest until they possess it! Of course,' her voice curdled with amusement, 'the fact they they're all quite handsome brutes does tend to give them an unfair advantage, especially where women are concerned!'

An odd feeling of lightheadedness made Sable stumble towards a nearby chair, her body folding up on it as her legs grew weak. There was something here she didn't understand. Something important, if not vital!'

'You say Rico showed you a photograph of me?' she asked a trifle breathlessly.

'That's right,' Ria agreed. 'A couple of years ago, shortly after I married Vitor he had to go away and leave me for a while, and he asked Ricardo to make sure no danger befell me in his absence. We became good friends and he confided in me how he intended to marry his godfather's daughter with her father's blessing, and that's when he produced your photograph as evidence of the joys that awaited him!' She laughed. 'I told him at the time that he was being impossibly chauvinistic if he expected someone as lovely as you to fall into his lap without a great deal of effort and wooing on his part! You can't believe how delighted I am that he took my lecture to heart.'

'Godfather's daughter . . .' Sable croaked, her mind

spinning with horror.

'Yes.' Ria sounded puzzled. 'Jaime Guimares, isn't it? Believe me, even before he'd met you Ricardo was adamant that he'd take you as his bride. I've never known a man so determined—with the exception of Vitor, of course . . .' Her voice tailed away reminiscently.

Sable stared down at the receiver as if it had lied to her. There was something dreadfully wrong here. *Ricardo* hadn't been the name of the man her father had mentioned as a prospective husband . . . and he'd described him as a contemporary—a boyhood friend . . . Sable pushed her hand despairingly through the dark wealth of her hair, as her anguished mind sought an explanation.

'Ria . . .' She moistened her lips nervously. 'Do you—do you know who Eurico and . . .' She searched her memory desperately for the other name, relaxing with a sigh when she recalled it. 'Eurico and Iolanda are?'

'Yes, of course.' Surprise was evidenced in Ria's immediate answer. 'They were Ricardo's parents. Iolanda died giving birth to him and Eurico was fatally injured in a riding accident about six years ago. Didn't you know?'

No, she hadn't known. Now she saw she must have misunderstood her father's angry attempt at an explanation. It hadn't been his friend Eurico he had lined up as her future bridegroom, but Eurico's son—Ricardo de Braganza!

The result was that she'd been duped, manipulated. Her fingers tightened round the receiver as she tried to come to terms with this shocking revelation. She'd been flushed from cover like a game bird, fooled into believing she was making her own choices and decisions when all the time she was being decoyed into a trap!

Only, thanks to the innocent chatter of his cousin's wife, she'd learned about Rico's heartless hypocrisy before she'd irrevocably surrendered her independence to him.

Somehow she gathered her reeling senses together sufficiently to waylay any suspicions the other girl might have had about her questions before replacing the receiver in its cradle.

Ria had spoken in all innocence, of that she was sure. Her intention presumably to flatter her new in-law with evidence of Rico's long-term interest in her. Obviously she'd assumed that Sable had been told of the relationship between her father and her newly taken husband. The fact that Rico had made no mention of knowing Jaime Guimares was all the proof she needed of his deviousness. This had certainly been no love-match on his part as she had begun to believe—only the exercise of a wilful determination not to be thwarted in a convenient plan!

Fortunately, at the eleventh hour she could still oppose him. In that instant all her previously subdued uncertainties crystallised into a solid decision. What was it Juliet had said about her unconsummated union with Romeo?—'Oh, I have bought the mansion of a love, but not possess'd it; and, though I am sold, not yet enjoyed.' Slowly she rose to her feet, her senses swimming as the shock of what she'd learned quickened her heartbeat dramatically.

Yes, that was it; and within its meaning lay her plan of immediate action. Ricardo de Braganza might have bought her with her father's deceitful connivance, and was most probably congratulating himself on the way he had fooled her into accepting a pre-conceived plan she had sworn never to be a party to. But she would make damn sure he would never enjoy her!

CHAPTER EIGHT

'THERE'S no need for you to bother—Rosina will help me change.' On the threshold of her bedroom Sable turned to face Rico, barring his entry with her body, her chin raised determinedly, her voice artificially controlled. During the past couple of hours before returning to change for the journey ahead she'd had plenty of time to dwell on the discovery of her husband's duplicity, the pain of his betrayal etching itself deeply into her whole being.

'Rosina won't thank you for being dragged from Aleixo's arms on the dance-floor,' he responded, mildly amused. 'Believe me, she's capitalising on your uncle's present mellowness to make her interest in that young man quite clear.'

'A situation for which you presumably claim most of the credit!' Sable remained where she was, her blue eyes accusing.

For a moment Rico's gaze lingered pensively on the unsteady curve of her lips, then he smiled. 'I should say both of us could claim equal credit in having defused a potentially explosive situation by turning it into circumstances which generated far less heat! The present state of affairs allows both of them to examine their own feelings without total commitment and in an environment acceptable to Rosina's father. A very satisfactory outcome, I should say.'

He reached across her, his hand brushing her shoulder as he pushed open the door. 'So in her absence, you will have to put up with my services, *meu amor*, unless, of course . . .' his cool, level gaze was unnerving, and she opened her mouth to protest further, before snapping it shut as he continued imperturbably '. . . you intend to arrive at our hotel still clad in your full wedding regalia?'

Sable turned, entering the room, feeling his dominating presence close behind her. Damn him! He knew perfectly well that she was unable to unfasten the tiny buttons at her back without help, and the alternative was not only unthinkable but impracticable, since unless she intended to spend the rest of her life clothed in white lace it would be to him she would have to turn for assistance eventually!

Her body held rigidly, she clenched her fists hard at her side as she felt his fingers begin their unhurried journey down her spine. He had lifted her hair, moving it over one shoulder to give him easy access to the small buttons, and she could feel his warm breath on her exposed neck as he bent diligently to his fiddly task.

If she hadn't steeled her heart against him she might have been amused at the thought of those large, masculine hands dealing with such a delicate process. As it was, she closed her eyes, praying her ordeal would soon be ended and he'd leave her alone to change into her going-away outfit.

One, two, three, four . . . She felt the buttons eased out of their holes, trying desperately to wrench her mind away from the pressure of his fingers against her sensitive skin. She could, of course, have refused to go anywhere with him. She could have ended their mockery of a marriage then and there. Only the thought of the local scandal such behaviour would create had stopped her. Roberto and Renata deserved better thanks for their affection and all the work they'd put in on her behalf than such a churlish action. In fact, her revenge might be even better the longer she allowed Rico to believe that he had found himself a tractable and compliant wife: the final reckoning more surprising and shocking!

Nine, ten, eleven, twelve . . . How many more were there? 'Ah!' she uttered a gasp of shock, her reflexes making her spring forward as warm lips touched her naked skin and a damp tongue tasted a waistline vertebra. Rico's low burst of laughter echoed in her ears as she spun round to face him.

'That's fine, thanks,' she managed unsteadily. 'I can finish by myself now.' She inched away from him, willing him to leave her in peace.

'If that's the way you want it . . .' His laconic murmur of agreement wasn't reflected in the sharp appraisal of his glinting eyes. 'If you change your mind, just give me a call. I'll wait for you in Luis's room.'

'Yes, fine . . . thank you,' she intoned breathlessly, delighted he hadn't tried to force the issue before she was ready for confrontation. 'I won't be long.'

Her whole body taut, she watched thankfully as, with one final, all-embracing look, he left her alone.

A pulse was hammering at the base of her throat, as quickly she unbuttoned the wrist fastenings and peeled the dress from her body. Pausing only long enough to place it on its padded hanger, she then discarded the long, layered half-slip that had given shape and body to the skirt. Wearing only a white satin bodyshaper and gossamer-fine nylon stockings, she reached inside the wardrobe for the silk two-piece she'd chosen in which to leave the reception, and afterwards for the flight to Rio.

The cream, fully lined, finely pleated skirt flared out just below her knees; the top, wide-necked and three-quarter-sleeved, rested just above hip level, her waist flattered by a self-coloured wide belt of the softest leather. Against the golden tan of her throat she wore a designer necklet of polished green jade set in gold, the soft lustre of the stone echoed in the high-heeled shoes that graced her slender feet.

Despite the warmth of the day she let her hair remain loose, contenting herself by brushing it back from her face to lie in a smooth fall to her shoulders. In fact her fingers were trembling so much in anticipation of the ordeal ahead of her that she doubted if she would have had the patience to confine its luxuriant growth into a more controlled style.

Repairing her make-up with a practiced hand, she took one long last look round the room she'd shared so happily with Rosina. There was only one way out of the trap into which she'd fallen, and that was to convince Rico that she would never be the kind of wife he demanded. She would give him no option but annulment or divorce, whichever was the simplest and quickest to obtain. In so doing she would undoubtedly alienate all her new-found family, who despite the recent more liberal laws still held to the old morality, where marriages were unbreakable contracts. It was unlikely, in the cicumstances she envisaged, that she'd ever be made welcome at the *hacienda* again.

It was a bitter price to pay. But not as bitter as the alternative of remaining shackled to a man who had made a contract with her father and had been resolved to see it honoured, come what may.

Closing her eyes while Rico chauffeured his own Mercedes for the hour's drive to the outskirts of the city, Sable leaned back on the soft upholstery, planning her strategy for the showdown that was imminent.

Entering their hotel room, her heart missed a beat as a quick glance round confirmed what she'd dreaded to see. Instead of two single beds, the pride of place was held by an enormous '*matrimonio*', covered in a gold-embossed quilt. Still, she recognised, thankfully there were also two large armchairs, apart from the normal bedroom furniture. Put together, they would make a comfortable resting place for the night for her once she'd convinced Rico that there was no way she intended to remain his wife.

'Well, *minha mulher* . . .'

As the door closed behind the porter, Rico moved like a panther to imprison her in his arms.

Only a few hours ago she would have melted beneath his overpowering embrace; now, her resolve hardened by the enormity of the masquerade in which he had acted, Sable's body froze in his arms as her graceful neck twisted away from his pleasure-seeking mouth.

'It's over, Rico. The pretence between us is finished. I know the truth,' she blurted out, drawing in a painful breath as his fingers moved to her arms, tightening against her soft flesh.

'What truth, Sable?' His eyes flickered at her obvious agitation, his fine mouth hardening, but his voice remained unflurried, conversational.

Mutely she moved her head, aware that his present coolness could evaporate in seconds at what she had to say.

'What truth, Sable?' he asked again, the silky tone in no way abating her apprehension.

'My father . . . you . . . the plans you made together. The way he offered me to you as some kind of concession because he was your godfather. The way you tricked me from the first moment you set eyes on me . . .' Anguish had sharpened her voice. 'Do I need to go on?'

'Relax, *meu amor*.' His dark eyes took a toll of her flushed face as his mouth curled in a wry smile. 'What's so dreadful about making a marriage that will delight your father?'

So it was true! For the first time she realised how much she'd been hoping against hope that Rico would deny it, would prove to her that he was at heart the carefree range-rider she had once supposed him, that Ria had been mistaken, that he'd acted spontaneously because he loved her . . .

Unable to free herself from his grip, she shivered, determined to oppose him, to make him face up to the reality of the situation.

'Everything about it's dreadful!' she stormed angrily. 'My father knew I wouldn't have anything to do with an arranged marriage. He told me he'd abandoned his plans before I agreed to come over here. Now I find out that the two of you have played me for a fool . . . railroading me into making a decision I never wanted to, by manoeuvring me into a situation that was none of my choice!'

The line of his mouth taut, he stared down at her defiant eyes.

'You're over-reacting, *querida*,' he told her softly. 'I imagine I owe Ria for this furious outburst . . .'

'Don't you dare blame her! How could she know your motives were so base that you'd lied to me from the start?' she interrupted fiercely.

'No lies, Sable!' he rejoined coolly. 'The most you can accuse me of is taking advantage of circumstances. You can hardly suppose your father or I had anything to do with Rosina's decision to elope or your own arbitrary action?'

'You're devious and unprincipled, and I detest you!' Sable's bitterness welled up inside her. With agonised eyes she stared at him. 'From the start you manipulated me, took advantage of my being a stranger in a country whose customs were alien to me . . .'

At the hollow note of defeat in her tone, Rico's brow furrowed.

'I seem to recall that it was you who announced your wish for an early wedding to your aunt.'

'Because of the way she looked at me . . . at us . . .' Sable choked back the lump in her throat. 'I felt humiliated.' She raised stormy eyes to Rico's quietly observant face. 'You intended this all along, didn't you, because you were determined not to see the joint plans you'd made with my father thwarted? You didn't even see me as a person—just as a commodity to be traded!'

She was breathing rapidly, her voice trembling but resolute. 'Well, you trapped me into marrying you, but I can't go through with it. The truth is that, despite everything, I still love Simon. If I can't have him, then I don't want anyone else.' Deliberately she falsified her feelings towards Simon in an effort to regain her pride, pausing as Rico's eyes hardened to match the implacability of his jaw, before ending defiantly, 'I was out of mind when I agreed to your proposal. Everything happened so quickly, otherwise I would have come to my senses before . . .'

'Before it was too late?' he bit out harshly. 'But now it is too late, *minha mulher*. It became so the moment the priest gave us his blessing.' There was a quiet menace in his voice. 'You are already my wife and that's what you shall remain. You may be able to twist your father round your little finger, God knows your mother was a mistress of the art, but I for one intend you shall face up to your responsibilities!'

'What do you know of my mother?' Even in her distress, Sable couldn't let the careless aspersion cast at Laura Guimares go unchallenged.

'Only that according to my own father she ruined

Jaime Guimares's life, dragging him around Europe
after her while she found escape from reality in a life of
false glamour. He gave up his country and his pride for
her—and received nothing in return—until you were
born.'

'How dare you speak about her like that?' Sable half
sobbed in her anger. 'She was a great artiste, everyone
loved her. But my father isn't very good at showing
affection, and he hated the adulation she received, he
was jealous of her admirers. He drove her away . . .' It
was the explanation she had made so often to herself to
explain Laura's desertion of them both.

'He was jealous of her *lovers*, Sable, and the last
thing he wanted was to see you accepting her standards.'

'And he thought marrying me off to you was the
answer!' She saw the flicker of rage darken his eyes, but
she was too far incensed to stop there. 'Well, you may
have taken advantage of my unhappiness to make a
successful takeover bid for a part of my father's assets,
but you'll find you haven't got such a bargain as you
expected, Senhor de Braganza!'

She turned on her heel, eyes blinded by furious tears,
stumbling a little on the high slender heels of her
beautiful shoes, intent on reaching the door and leaving
the room to go anywhere away from the dark,
thunderous face of the man who'd listened to her final
denunciation in bodeful silence.

When a strong arm curled round her waist to half lift,
half carry her to the bed, she opened her mouth to
shriek, only to have her incipient cry stifled in her throat
as Rico's body pinned her to the soft mattress, his
mouth covering her own with irresistible intent.

Powerful and thrusting, he claimed her mouth for his
own with none of the finesse she had grown accustomed
to. Her head thrust into the pillow, fiercely

determined to oppose him, she concentrated on trying to expel his dominant invasion, hardly aware that with his having trapped her into position with one long, muscular leg, his hands were free to slip the catch of her belt and to push the fine silk top upward, pulling it from her arms to free her satin-covered breasts.

As soon as she realised his purpose she tried to shake off the yoke of his restraining body, momentarily relieved when he brought the passionate, devouring kiss to an end. Her respite was to be short-lived, as with deadly purpose Rico lowered the thin straps of the glamorous bodyshaper, drawing it down to her waist, urgent fingers pushing it still further, taking with it the silken pleats of the elasticated-waist skirt.

Sable fought silently, all her senses focused on escaping the threat of the powerful male body that was so easily overpowering her, gasping aloud as Rico's avid lips closed around her mulberry-tipped breasts in turn, bringing them to a tumescent fulfilment in the warmth of his mouth.

Now she found her voice and a thin moan escaped her parted lips, desire racing unbidden along sensitive nerve-endings, her silky skin quivering, horribly aware that her body was betraying her will, responding to the physical stimulus lavished on it by the purposeful man she'd married and tried to deny.

When the inexorably ravishing hands moved to caress her thighs, to taunt and tease the satin skin that flailed helplessly beneath them, she knew, as surely he must too, that her body was offering only token resistance, the heated, quivering flesh unable to hide its reaction to the practised hands that relentlessly cajoled its response. He would take her, and as he mastered her she would cry with joy as her frustration dissolved, because Rico was her husband, the man she'd wanted to love, the man she'd wanted to trust and for so brief a time she could hold that tarnished image bright and welcome him. But afterwards . . . A broken sob escaped her lips. Dear God . . what of afterwards? She turned her head sideways into the pillow, all struggle vanquished.

When Rico moved and she could feel the coolness of the air-conditioning a balm against her bared, burning flesh, she supposed he'd paused to rid himself of the encumbrance of his own clothing. Her mouth throbbing, her body unsatiated and pulsating with an inner beat over which she seemed to have no control, she stirred on the pillow, lifting her head to seek him, an aching need spurring her to witness his beautiful, positive, masculine body before it overwhelmed her.

He was standing, fully clothed, staring down at her as she scrambled her legs beneath her, reaching for the jumble of clothes at the foot of the bed, holding them against herself to shield her trembling body from his all-embracing stare. Her breath rasping between her lips, she searched that dark face for some emotion but found none. Savage lines of strain grooved his taut cheeks, and his eyes were cold and empty like the Arctic *tundra*.

'Not such a bad bargain after all . . .' He was breathing heavily, a dusky flush on the high cheekbones. 'With a little more encouragement . . .' His eyes narrowed, passing in what she assessed as contemptuous regard from her tumbled hair to the neatly varnished toes of her slim feet. 'With a little more encouragement you may find I make a very good substitute for your playboy lover.'

She'd been mad to taunt him. Any newly married man would have reacted unfavourably to her agonised attestation. It wasn't necessary to be Brazilian and brought up in the code of *machismo* for a man to react so violently, but it helped. Yet defiantly Sable refused to acknowledge aloud her own culpability for what had occurred.

'You brute!' she derided, her voice low-pitched, shaking with fury.

'No.' Rico was remarkably calm as he corrected her. 'A brute would have torn every stitch of clothing from you and taken what is by right his to command. On the contrary, I have preserved your wardrobe and respected, for the time being, your wish to repulse me.'

'And I'm supposed to be grateful?' He had humiliated her. Probably he was laughing secretly at the erotic tricks he had played on her unsuspecting flesh; almost certainly he was not unaware of how successful they'd been.

'If not grateful, at least civil,' he told her, sternly remote. 'However much you resent the fact that Jaime Guimares is my godfather, there's nothing that can be done about it, or about our marriage—at least not in the near future, as you will be well aware when you've calmed down. Tomorrow we go to Rio. I suggest if you wish to enjoy everything it offers you keep a check on your hostility.'

She hesitated, recognising the sense in what he said but uncertain of how he saw their immediate relationship. 'Rico . . .' She swallowed, gathering together the remnants of her courage which had been disseminated by the storm of her arousal. 'I won't change my mind. I want you to promise me . . .'

A small, humourless smile turned the corner of his mouth as her blue gaze searched the harsh planes of his face for reassurance.

The dark head shook slowly. 'No promises, Sable. Only an assurance that, like most men, I find the ultimate joy and excitement of possessing a woman is in mutual enjoyment.' He paused meaningfully. 'And I have no intention of disturbing your sleep tonight, so if you had any idea about sleeping in one of the chairs—forget it.' His smile deepened, became more natural as her long lashes dropped to mask the surprise his correct diagnosis of her intentions had provoked. 'Do we understand each other, *querida*?' he asked softly.

Torn by indecision, grieved by the way she'd been bartered between two powerful men, temporarily beaten but unbowed, Sable nodded her consent.

'Good. In that case you'll forgive me if I spend an hour or so in the bar downstairs to restore my good temper!' He flashed her a gleaming smile that for a brief, inexplicable second turned her heart, and then he was gone, closing the door quietly behind him.

What was she supposed to make of that? she asked herself wearily, dragging her exhausted limbs towards the luxurious bathroom. That he intended to drown his sorrows in alcohol, or find release for his overheated emotions with a woman whose profession it was to assuage such needs with pretended passion?

Why should she care, anyway? She brushed a tear from her cheek. Her world had already collapsed around her. But all was not lost yet. Tomorrow she'd be in Rio, the magical city of lights and colour and carnival. The glittering social capital of Brazil, where her mother, the fabulous Laura Armstrong, had captured the heart of thousands with her style, her wit and her lovely voice.

If Rico had loved her, even *liked* her, she would have willingly abandoned her aspirations to emulate her mother, accepting that the needs of her husband and his estate would offer her at least as equal a challenge.

Now she had nothing, and perhaps the time had come to re-examine her old ambitions. To test her talent in the same crucible from which Laura Guimares had emerged to glitter with such eminence . . . Turning on the taps, she stepped into the bath, allowing the warm water to refresh her, washing away the taint of Rico's persuasive hands, his voracious lips. She smiled to herself as new hope was born within her. Somehow she would get through the hours until an opportunity presented itself, or she could create one. Then she would escape from the bondage into which she'd been so blindly driven and make a new life for herself!

It was half-past three in the afternoon when the VASP Boeing 747 touched down at Rio's international airport. Descending from its air-conditioned interior on to the steps leading to the tarmac, Sable found herself gasping as the heat bounced back to meet her.

'Are you all right?' Rico, who had preceded her down the steps, took her arm to assist her to the ground.

'Thank you, yes,' she answered him politely, moving away from his supporting arm. 'I guess I didn't expect quite such a change of temperature!'

'You've just flown over the Tropic of Capricorn—temperatures are always high here—summer and winter.' He made no attempt to regain physical contact with her. 'It's generally cooler down south in Rio Grande do Sul. We even get frost there sometimes in the winter.' He glanced at her set profile as she walked beside him. 'I hope Rio will come up to all your expectations of it.'

'You don't care for it yourself?' Something in his tone had warned her this might be the case, as she continued their civil conversation. However turbulent her feelings towards Rico, there was nothing to be gained by carrying their feud into public. If she were to accomplish her plans, she must antagonise him as little as possible in the short time they would be together.

'For a short holiday, it's fine.' He shrugged. 'But to my mind surfing at Copacabana can't compare with riding across the *pampas*. I'm afraid I find the loneliness of the rolling plains much more to my liking than the crowded beaches of the city.'

'But all the excitement is here!' Sable protested. 'All the glamour and entertainment . . .'

'And all the poverty and corruption. The *favelas* of the city look pretty enough from a distance, but they're not included on any tourist itinerary . . .'

'I'm not going to let you spoil it for me!' Sable turned accusing eyes towards the man at her side.

'Nor do I intend to.' He returned her look calmly. 'My only purpose for coming here is for your pleasure. Wait here—I'm going to the luggage-collection bay.'

Without giving her the chance to comment, Rico stroke away, leaving her standing there surrounded by a throng of chattering people. As her eyes scanned the crowd, taking in every detail, she found her mind drifting back to earlier events.

Incredibly, she'd been asleep when Rico had returned in what must have been the early hours of the morning, and she had no recollection of his having spent the night beside her. Finding the bed empty when she'd awakened had been an unexpected bonus, and when Rico had emerged fully clothed from the adjoining bathroom and told her he'd see her in fifteen minutes' time in the breakfast room, leaving her without even a peck on the cheek as a greeting, she'd been relieved.

The journey from the airport was accomplished in comparative silence as Rico concentrated on negotiating the packed roads in the hired Mercedes he'd arranged to collect, while Sable stared out of the window at the colourful scenes all around her.

'Where are we staying?' she ventured at last as he manoeuvred the expensive car neatly between two Volkswagens seemingly determined to cut him up.

'Oh, I don't think you'll be disappointed, Sable. I thought as our time was limited we'd do it in style. I've booked us into one of Rio's most famous hotels overlooking Copacabana, with the mountains and Corcovado with its famous statue of Christ the Redeemer as a backdrop. I think you'll like it.'

It had to be the understatement of the year, Sable thought as she caught her first sight of the famous beach, its sand white against the pure blue of the sea. Even the two three-lane roads that separated it from the uninterrupted line of glistening white hotels did little to mar its natural beauty.

A wild excitement beat in her heart, a feeling that at last she was in touch with her destiny. Minutes later they had reached their destination, traversed the luxurious reception area, obtained their key and were on their way upwards.

'But this is the bridal suite!' Alone in the room with Rico, their luggage neatly racked by the porter, Sable met his sombre gaze with wide-eyed apprehension.

'Of course.' He agreed easily. 'It seemed apt—at the time I booked it.' He shrugged broad shoulders, looking round the room with every sign of approval, noting the flowers, the luxurious fittings and the ice-bucket of champagne beside the bed. 'And will undoubtedly prove to be so, before the week is out.'

His tone was light but meaningful as he walked across to the bucket and withdrew the bottle, glancing at the label before beginning to undo the wires that secured the cork.

'I don't want anything to drink,' she protested, her

heart hammering with the strength of the fear that assailed her, as she stared at the dark head bent intently over the self-imposed task. 'Rico, please . . .' Her voice sawed with effort. 'Nothing has changed. You know how I feel. I only came here with you because I didn't want to cause a scandal at home on my wedding day. I hoped when we were alone together we could discuss the future—reasonably . . . Oh!' Her sentence was terminated with a shriek as the cork shot out of the bottle and hit the ceiling.

Lifting the two long, slender glasses in what appeared to be practised fingers, Rico filled each with the foaming liquid before replacing the bottle in the ice and coming towards her.'

'Champagne will steady your nerves.' He held out a glass to her, watching her intently as she reluctantly accepted it, raising it to her lips to take a refreshing mouthful. 'As for discussing our future, as far as I'm concerned, it's already settled. When we leave Rio, I shall take you back with me to Ribatejo.' His dark eyes dwelt on her pale face. 'The sooner you resign yourself to that fact, the better it will be for you, *meu amor*. You can't expect either your father or your uncle to deny your married state and offer you a roof over your head, so you're in no position to bargain with me, even if I were prepared to listen.'

Sable's fingers tightened round the slender stem of her glass, afraid of Rico's superior strength, knowing it could command her physical submission with the same consummate ease as it had demolished her at tennis. But she was under no illusions. This was no game. This time Rico's self-respect as a man was at stake.

She shivered spontaneously. To a man like her husband her rebellion would pose a formidable challenge, and she couldn't discount the possibility that he might use violence to subdue her if she tried his patience too far. On the other hand, she suspected he might be master of more subtle arts in his determination to conquer her resistance . . .

'Isabella . . .' Sable started at his usage of her baptismal name, as Rico's voice broke into her troubled thoughts, and he took her glass from her nerveless grip, reaching behind him to place it on an adjacent table. 'The important thing is that we *are* married—not the complicated pathways that led us to that decision.' He paused. 'Is it really so bad that your father approves of me—or . . .' his eyes narrowed thoughtfully 'was your decision to wed me motivated by a desire to revenge yourself on him for what you saw as his villainy?'

'Whatever my motives, I regret them now,' she told him tonelessly. Useless to speak to him in terms of love when all he understood were desire and determination.

'Then regret must be your bed-fellow, *meu amor*.' The endearment reeked of sarcasm as firm hands on her shoulders commanded her attention. Through the thin cream silk of her two-piece she could feel the dry warmth of his palms as he fixed her wide blue eyes with his intent scrutiny. 'Make no mistake about it, Sable, you *are* my wife and that is what you'll remain. The sooner you accept that as a fact, the happier we'll both be!'

He moved away, reaching once more for the champagne bottle, while she stared down at her tightly clasped hands. Regret would indeed be her bed-fellow. But Rico—never!

CHAPTER NINE

SABLE stirred, stretched and opened her eyes. The large room was in partial darkness. Only an area at the far end of the extensive, graciously furnished space was illuminated. Pulling herself upright into a sitting position, her eyes becoming accustomed to the dimness, she saw Rico lounging on a cream leather chaise-longue, ostensibly immersed in the pages of a thick magazine.

How long had she been asleep? A spasm of alarm surged through her. And what had been happening? She remembered accepting a second glass of champagne, partly because she recognised that the less she provoked Rico over small matters the easier life would be for her, and partly because its stimulus helped to sustain her courage. She frowned. Had there been yet a further glass after that? Her tongue traced the outline of her lips. They certainly felt very dry, and her mouth was parched. She had a faint recollection of beginning to feel sleepy and stretching back on the pillows—and then—nothing!

'Ah—you're awake at last.' The tall figure of her husband unwound, laid down the magazine and strolled towards her across the expanse of carpeted floor. 'I was going to give you another fifteen minutes and then I was going to find some means of awakening you gently.' The gleam in his eyes suggested he wouldn't have had to search far for such a remedy.

'How long have I been asleep?' She swung her legs off the bed, conscious now of the pangs of hunger, and ran her fingers through her rumpled hair.

Rico shrugged. 'Long enough to get over the effects of half a bottle of vintage champagne, I hope.' He smiled at her pleasantly. 'And also long enough to have discovered a healthy appetite, I trust. This hotel has reputedly one of the finest restaurants in Brazil, and I've arranged for us to have a table next to a window so you can enjoy a panoramic view of the city while you're eating.' He glanced down at his gold watch. 'Do you think you could be ready in thirty minutes?'

'Of course!' Sable scrambled to her feet, finding the prospect of food as enticing as that of mingling in public rather than staying in the close confines of the room. 'I'm sorry if I've kept you waiting to eat—I don't usually sleep in the late afternoon,' she offered graciously, praying that his apparent good humour would endure for the rest of the evening.

'Don't apologise, Sable, there's a lot to be said for the practice of *siesta*. It can be extended to include some of life's most pleasurable experiences.' He moved away from her to switch on a series of wall-lights which gave the room a soft, intimate glow. 'Besides,' he continued smoothly, 'my time wasn't entirely wasted; apart from the pleasure of watching you asleep and being able to appreciate your beauty without interruption, you'll find I've already unpacked your cases for you, and selected a dress for you to wear tonight.'

'That wasn't necessary . . .' Torn between annoyance and embarrassment that he'd dared to touch her personal belongings, she felt the warm blood rise in her cheeks.

'Perhaps not,' he agreed imperturbably. 'It was, however, a very pleasurable occupation, and the clothes have doubtless benefited by being released from such cramped confinement.' He moved with effortless masculine grace towards one of the large fitted wardrobes adjacent to the bed, removing a hanger on which she saw suspended the scarlet dress she'd worn to the dance at the Country Club.

'However, I took the precaution of having this one pressed for you so you can wear it for me tonight.'

Against his own light cream trousers and pastel silk shirt, the dress hung like a matador's *muleta*—a vibrant, teasing splash of colour. Seeing the strong tanned hands that grasped the hanger, Sable experienced a mental picture of those same predatory fingers sorting their way through her case, touching the exquisite silk and chiffon lingerie she had spoiled herself with when she had been existing on the generous allowance her father made her.

She squirmed as if the hands that had touched her intimate garments had taken their liberties on her own body. It was almost in self-defence that she rejected his idea, refuting his right to make any selection on her behalf.

'That old thing?' She disowned her own affection for the garment. 'Oh, no, I shan't wear that!'

'I think you will, *meu amor*.' There was nothing about his calm voice to alarm her, yet Sable found herself unable to control a frisson of apprehension in response to his simple statement. 'I've already complied with your wishes once this evening; now it's your turn to oblige me.' He offered the dress to her.

For a moment she hesitated. Was she supposed to read a threat into those carefully chosen words? Toying with the idea of defying him for the pure pleasure of it, she changed her mind at the last second, reminding herself that caution and compliance must be her bywords until she could free herself from his surveillance. There was little point in fighting a battle when she was the one with the most to lose!

'Oh, very well—if it means that much to you . . .' She took the hanger from his hand with every sign of bad grace. 'Though why you would want me to wear this when I've far more suitable dresses . . .' She flicked a disgruntled glance at him.

'*Why*, my beautiful wife?' A sudden fire flamed in his dark eyes. 'The reason is very simple. It's what you wore when you accepted my offer of marriage. Hopefully it may remind you of that assent! Besides,' his lips twisted into a smile, 'it suits you very well. You look like a gypsy—colourful, passionate and defiant . . .'

'If it's defiance you want . . .' Forgetting her earlier resolve, she made to discard the dress, but he was too quick for her.

'Only if you are prepared to defend it to the final score!' His hand locked round her wrist, pulling her towards him. 'Are you, Sable?' he asked softly.

'I—I don't want to fight you.' The words were forced out of her in her own defence, as her heart hammered in protest at his nearness. Once more she experienced the disturbing sensation that stirred her whenever Rico came close to her. She could feel it racing through her, stimulating her to the unwilling awareness of the needs her body clamoured to satisfy, but which her pride would never permit.

If Rico had loved her, she would have welcomed the revelation, but he'd trapped her . . . made her his prisoner . . . The burning resentment of which he'd been the architect flared up anew inside her.

'I'll wear whatever pleases you—just let me go!'

She'd half expected him to seal her unconditional surrender by making her accept another of those searching kisses which left her weak-kneed and trembling, and felt almost disappointed when he released her instantly, thereby denying her the opportunity of adding another figure to the score already held against him, giving her instead a little push towards the bathroom, and an admonition not to keep him waiting.

It was two in the morning when Rico escorted her from the foyer of the nightclub where they'd spent the last part of the evening. She staggered slightly as she reached the pavement, still exhilarated by the wild exuberance of the last dance she'd performed, held a close captive in Rico's arms. A passionate, wanton performance in which he'd matched her for speed and dexterity and outshone her in pure stamina, so that their fellow dancers had actually moved aside on the tiny dance-floor, allowing them the space to move. And, as the band had climaxed on a crescendo and she'd collapsed dramatically against the strong frame of Rico's body, they had greeted the end of their unrehearsed exhibition with warm applause.

For those few moments of total abandon she'd forgotten the problems she faced, aware only that the beat of the drums and the speed of the rhythm were acting like a catharsis on her beleaguered spirit, offering her a way to release her pent-up anger and pain. Now, as the cooler night air struck her heated skin, she was forcibly reminded that the evening was not by any means ended.

As Rico's arm moved quickly round her waist to steady her, Sable found herself flinching, trying to evade both his touch and the delicate, tangy aroma of an expensive cologne. Whatever she did, she mustn't give him the slightest grounds for supposing she had changed her mind! Yet it was impossible to deny how much she'd enjoyed herself. For those few hours she'd forgotten that she was an unwilling captive, delighting in every new experience to which her attractive escort had introduced her. And Rico *was* attractive. She would have to be blind or insane not to admit it and, heaven knew, she was neither. Just wounded and furious.

What had her father said to her? 'Physical attributes in a man are no guarantee of a good marriage.' Tonight, after they had left the restaurant, Rico had been the perfect escort, charming and attentive, and for a short while she had dropped her guard, blossoming beneath his courteous attention, aware that other women in the room had looked more than once at his lean-muscled body and prepossessing face. But her father had been right. In themselves, good looks were meaningless. Whatever happened she mustn't allow herself to be seduced by outward appearances, mustn't submit to a man guided only by his physical appetite, and an eye to a good bargain. Her worst enemy was going to be the curious mixture of fierce antagonism and vibrant attraction that took control of her whenever her autocratic husband came within feet of her!

She uttered a soft cry of protest as Rico's hand tightened round her waist in answer to her involuntary movement, and he drew her closer to his own lean body. 'Tired, sweet wife? Ready for bed at last?' he enquired pleasantly.

It was as if someone had emptied a bag of ice-cubes down her back, and she couldn't prevent the shudder that traversed her spine at the softly suggestive words. Somhow she had to survive the night without allowing the dominant man at her side the rights he so arrogantly claimed over her. If she could achieve that, tomorrow she could make her final move. Already a plan had formed in her mind. Tomorrow . . . but the prospect of the coming night loomed over her with the menace of a forest fire.

'I guess I'm more tired than I thought. I feel quite sleepy now.' She forced herself to smother a make-believe yawn. Hadn't she read somewhere that it was impossible for a man to make love to a woman who was sick, asleep or had a broken leg?

'I had a feeling you might,' Rico observed drily, leading her leisurely towards the car park. 'Fortunately our time's our own, so you can sleep in late tomorrow morning.'

'Oh, that would be a shame!' Sable sank down into the comfort of the car as Rico closed the door behind her, waiting for him to take his place in the driver's seat before adding with a contrived eagerness, 'I was hoping to go on a tourist's tour of the city by day, starting with an early-morning swim.'

'I'm sure that could be arranged.' He looked at her curiously as he started the car into motion, obviously intrigued by her sudden animation.

'And afterwards can we go up the Sugar Loaf by cable car?'

'Why not?' He tossed her an amused glance. 'And we can to to the top of Corcovada too, if you like. It's twice the height of Sugar Loaf, and from its summit there's an unforgettable view of the city.'

'Lovely.' Sable sank down into the soft upholstery of the Mercedes, drawing her light angora stole closer round her shoulders, as a sudden cold shiver teased her flesh. Rico was in an affable mood—which had been her aim. Please, God—let him stay that way!

Thirty minutes later she was waiting for him to unlock the door of their room, her whole body now enveloped in a cold chill of apprehension.

'May I use the bathroom first?' She was on her way across the large room, without waiting for an answer.

'Yes, *querida*, you may, but not just yet.' Rico had moved even faster, overtaking her and grasping her upper arms, pulling her into his embrace.

'Please,' she lied despairingly. 'My need's desperate!'

'Not as desperate as mine!' Rico told her thickly, the palms of his hands moving erotically against her shoulder-blades, sending crazy waves of sensation trembling down her spine. 'Have you any idea what it's been like for me this evening—just being with you, watching you move and eat and smile? 'You're like a fire in my blood, *minha querida*—feel me, I'm burning up for you.' He took one of the hands she'd raised in a vain effort to ward him off and held its palm to his cheek. 'The sight, the scent, the feel of you . . .' He dragged her hand across his mouth, burning the palm with the brand of his lips.

His hoarse whisper tortured her sensibilities, as every female instinct in her screamed its need to console him and enjoy the satisfaction she dared not seek. But to give in, to satisfy his lust for her would put her on a par with the *raparigas* she'd glimpsed parading outside some of the more gaudily lighted clubs, and destroy her plans for the future.

'Nothing's changed, Rico.' Her words came quickly as she quashed her own instincts, blindingly aware that the pleasant evening they'd spent together had only been the lull before the storm, despite her efforts to continue the calm. 'I don't want to be your wife—now or ever.'

'And I told you, you have no choice!' he remonstrated thickly. '*Mai de Deus*, Sable! It's time you grew up and behaved like an adult. God knows, I've been patient with you, but I warn you—don't try me too far—I'm only human!'

The evidence of that fact was disturbingly apparent as he pulled her reluctant body against his own.

'So am I!' she retorted furiously. 'And that gives me the right of freedom of choice.'

'Freedom of choice, yes!' The grimness of his tone assaulted her ears. 'But wilful and continuing opposition to consummating our marriage for no good reason—no, Sable. This is a right I'm not prepared to allow you.' he stared down into her mutinous face. 'Our marriage was a legal contract, and no one breaks a contract made with me without incurring the severest penalties.'

'Impose your penalties, then,' she shot back at him, meeting his dark regard with a fierce pride as she rose to the implicit challenge of his words. 'None can be as punitive as being forced to live with you when I'm still in love with Simon!'

'*Mai de Deus!*' He uttered the oath feelingly, pushing her rigid body away from him with such force that she stumbled backwards, subsiding on to the bed. 'Anyone would think you were bound and gagged and dragged to the altar blindfold!'

'I was certainly blind,' she taunted him. 'You knew how I felt about an arranged marriage. You knew I wouldn't ever marry anyone my father chose for me! You deliberately kept the knowledge of who you were and the plans you and my father had made from me. Do you expect me to be happy about that?'

'Why not?' He looked down haughtily at her angry face. 'At least I'm not the elderly widower you supposed had been chosen as your partner.' His eyes held hers, dark and incredibly dangerous as he moved towards her. 'It's about time you grew up, Sable, and faced facts. You're beyond the age when young girls nurture impossible romantic fantasies. It's not necessary to be in love to make love, and I have no intention of accepting a platonic marriage.' He heaved in a an angry breath. 'At an age when other men were seeking brides I was fully occupied in keeping control of Ribatejo, content that in England there was the daughter of a man I loved and respected, who would be brought to meet me when the time was right. Now, I *have* met her and she is my wife . . .'

'Only because you chose to ask her at a time she was emotionally unstable, and had no idea it was the culmination of a well-planned campaign!' Sable flung back at him unbearably provoked by his unbending attitude, and throwing caution to the winds.

'Every successful courtship is a well-planned campaign!' Rico's voice was harshly censorious, as vexation tightened a band of steel round Sable's heart.

'But not every one is based on deceit! I had the right to know exactly who you were and the tacit agreement you had with my father. If you'd been honourable you would have told me at the start!'

'And let your wilfulness and prejudice blind you to reality?' he demanded brutally. 'I didn't want you hampered by your own myopia where your father is concerned.'

'Because you knew I would never have agreed to an alliance based on an understanding to which I had never been made a party!' Her eyes flashed blue fire. 'Why won't you be honest with yourself, Rico? All we have is a paper marriage that will bring joy to neither of us.' She paused to control the rising spiral of her voice, before continuing her words throbbing with passion. 'Rico, please—can't you see? I want more out of life than just being kept and well cared for and filling a place in the society in which you circulate; and you—you deserve to have a wife who will love you and honour you . . .'

'And obey me?' The softness of the question wasn't echoed in the dark glitter of his eyes. 'But those are the promises *you* made, *meu amor*, and if you didn't mean to keep them then you should have considered their meaning more deeply before committing yourself.' His voice deepened its crisp tones, offering her no mercy. 'Listen to me, Sable, because this is the last time I'm prepared to discuss the subject. Ribatejo needs legitimate heirs . . .' He reached towards her, pulling her roughly to her feet. 'And it is you, Senhora de Braganza, who will provide them for me—willingly by preference, but unwillingly if necessary!'

He reached out a hand and, ignoring the nervous way she jerked away from his burning touch, drew it with a contained gentleness down one side of her face while she returned his appraisal with empty eyes, her worst fears realised. Then he released her, his broad shoulders moving in a careless shrug. 'After that requirement has been met you'll be free to spend the rest of your life mourning your actor lover without any further attempt from me to dissuade you.' He paused meaningfully, then added softly, 'That is the greatest concession I'm prepared to make, so you'd do well to sleep on it!'

Silently she watched him walk towards the curtained windows leading to the balcony, as his words drifted back to her. 'Get ready for bed. We've a heavy schedule of sightseeing ahead of us tomorrow, and we both need a good night's rest.'

She had survived. That was the thought she must cling to as she fought to control the rapid beating of her heart. She'd gained another night's respite, but clearly Rico intended it to be the last one. She'd tried to reason with him, even at this late hour preferring to get the marriage dissolved through mutual agreement, rather than take the alternative steps she'd planned. Wearily she headed for the bathroom. If she were to escape before the consummation of their marriage made it morally difficult for her to do so, and legally more problematical to obtain a dissolution, then she had no other option.

The following morning Sable awakened refreshed by her sleep and filled with a tremulous excitement about what she intended to do. It had been several hours before she'd managed to find release from her tension in slumber, too aware of Rico's taut body beside her in the wide bed to be able to relax completely. But she'd put the time to good purpose, finalising the plan of action she'd already devised.

During their tour of the city the night before, they'd passed the nightclub where her mother had performed under her maiden name of Laura Armstrong. Elegant and expensive, it was just the kind of establishment she could envisage herself appearing in. Naturally, the main artistes would be booked many months in advance, but there were bound to be minor spots . . . And even though it was a long time ago, Laura had been a big star, and her name would surely give her daughter an entrée?

The traveller's cheques she'd brought with her for personal expenses had been over-generous and hardly touched. If she found cheap lodgings and budgeted carefully she would have enough money to last her through the difficult early days while she was trying to get herself established. The main problem had always been how she could escape from Rico's supervision long enough to give her a good head start. But even that hurdle had been cleared in the small hours of the morning, she congratulated herself with satisfaction. Rio was a large city. Once lost in its labyrinth of streets, she was quietly confident she could stay hidden.

Besides, she'd comforted herself, Rico would have too much pride to go looking for a woman who so

obviously didn't want to have anything to do with him.
No, she reasoned, he would finally see there was no
future for them together and cut his losses. It would be
the only sensible thing to do, and Rico's head ruled his
heart any day, didn't it?

'Ah, awake already—good!' The subject of her
thoughts emerged from the bathroom, stripped to the
waist, and smiled down at her, for all the world as if
there had never been that violent exchange of words and
ideas the previous night. 'If you still want to go for a
swim this morning, the sooner we start the better. By ten
you won't be able to put a pin between the sunbathers
on Copacabana or Ipanema.' His smile deepened as
Sable watched him warily, astonished that he could
behave as if nothing was wrong between them. 'In fact,'
he continued lazily, 'the best plan would be for us to
drive further along the coast to Leblon—not so
fashionable, but equally beautiful, I think you'll agree.'

'Whatever you think best,' she found herself
agreeing, irritated to find her pulse beginning to gather
pace as Rico's muscled shoulders shrugged themselves
int a cotton T-shirt. 'Are—are the plans we made last
night still on?'

'Of course.' He managed to sound surprised. 'Unless
you want to change your mind.'

'No—no,' she hastened to assure him, reaching for
her wrap. She scrambled out of bed and tied the sash
firmly round her slender waist. 'I'm looking forward to
seeing Rio.'

What had she expected? she asked herself later as she
brushed her dark hair before securing it with a clasp at
her neck. More recriminations? A black temper?
Certainly not the pleasant greeting she had been
accorded. But then, she told herself grimly, Rico's

complaisance sprang from his confidence that the last word had been spoken about their relationship—and that he had had it! Despite the warmth of the morning, she shivered. Fortunately she wouldn't be around when he discovered just how wrong that surmise had been.

It wasn't until they'd returned to their hotel for lunch after a morning spent on the glorious beach of Leblon, followed by an extensive tour of the city, that Sable was able to put the first part of her plan into action.

While Rico was showering she packed a few basic clothes, her jewellery and personal papers into a holdall and slipped outside the room, taking it swiftly downstairs into the lobby, asking the receptionist to look after it for an hour or so.

Pulse racing, heart pounding with anxiety, she regained the room seconds before Rico emerged clad only in dark briefs, his black hair glistening with moisture, his tanned skin smooth and fresh-smelling.

'I thought we might go to the botanical gardens after lunch, or perhaps you'd prefer the beach again, or even . . .' his voice deepened 'stay here and have a siesta, hmm?'

'I—I . . .' Now the time had come, Sable was seized with an almost paralytic fear. But it was what she wanted, wasn't it? There was no way she could stay with this autocratic, demanding man who seemed to think it was only a matter of time before his persistence wore her down. She swallowed, lifting her hand to drag her fingers through its dark tangle. 'As a matter of fact, there's an excellent beauty shop in the hotel. I phoned them while you were getting ready. I thought I might go and have a facial and get my hair done when we've eaten.'

'Gilding the lily?' Indulgence and blatant masculine approval mingled in the steady gaze that drifted the length of her body before returning with a quizzical smile to her face.

So much depended on his approval! Try as she might, it was impossible to control the slight tremble in her voice. 'My skin's not used to this heat.' She raised tentative fingers to touch her cheek. 'I need advice about a moisturiser, and my hair needs trimming and conditioning . . .'

'Does it?' He came so close to her that she drew in her breath in an abortive attempt to steel herself against her reaction to his nearness. One hand lifted a raven tress speculatively before releasing it, moving to her face to drift gentle fingers down her cheek. Heat rose to meet it as a flush of shame at her deception added impact to the evidence of the sun's caress.

'What drives you to make yourself even more beautiful, I wonder? Do you think my self-control is not already stretched to its limit?'

'Rico . . .' She breathed his name, ashamed that the deep timbre of his voice could thrill through her resistance, turning her blood to fire.

'Sable . . .'

She melted in his arms, closing her eyes, lifting her hands to his naked shoulders as he reached for her. The coolness of his skin was misleading, for his mouth scorched her like fire, drawing an answering thread of passion from her eager lips. This was 'goodbye'. The last time she'd ever be in his arms, although Rico didn't know it. Strangely, there was regret mixed with the excitement of her resolve.

As Rico's hands followed the slender lines of her body, she could feel his strong frame trembling.

'Sable—open your eyes and look at me,' he instructed hoarsely.

Unwillingly she did so, unnerved by the blazing

intensity in his lean face.

'Forget about lunch—forget about your hair—stay with me here—now. You want me as much as I want you. It's only your stubborn pride that prevents you from admitting it!' There was a febrile glitter in his midnight eyes that terrified her. It would be so easy—and so wrong, when deep in her heart she knew that a marriage based on sexual attraction alone would be as hollow and empty as that of her parents!

'Rico—I'm starving,' she protested prettily, her heart in her mouth, as she played for time. 'And the sun's given me a slight headache, but it'll go when I've eaten, and I always find it soothing to have my hair dressed. By this evening I'll be fine.'

'Is that a guarantee?' he asked softly, his meaning unequivocal, and she knew her time limit had definitely expired.

'Definitely,' she answered honestly in a low voice.

He stood away from her, his expression enigmatic as she passed him on light steps, making for the bathroom, pausing at the door. 'I'll only be a few minutes.'

It was in fact ten minutes later when she emerged, showered, dressed in a cool cotton dress, with her composure restored, to take lunch snack-style by the hotel's swimming pool, washing down the light salad and fruit with a dry white wine.

At three o'clock she made the move that was going to redirect the path of her life. Casually rising to her feet, she looked down at Rico's lounging figure.

'It's time for my appointment.' The words sounded odd as they issued from her unnaturally dry mouth.

Dark eyes raised lethargically from the book he'd been reading. 'I'll wait for her here. Be beautiful, *minha* Isabella.'

It was an odd farewell for a final parting, and one she

knew she'd never forget.

Hastening to the large reception hall, she sat down at one of the many tables, drawing towards herself a piece of hotel letter-headed paper and taking her own gold ballpoint from her bag. She'd been quiet over lunch, aware of Rico's curious glances, but ignoring them as she wrestled with the problem of the form her final letter to him should take.

In the end she kept it brief: telling him that, as he knew, she'd never intended to fulfil her vows. Her destiny lay elsewhere and she was taking steps to accomplish it. If he would arrange for the clothes she'd left to be kept at the hotel, she'd make arrangements to have them collected when she was settled. She hoped he would take urgent steps to get their marriage annulled, using her letter as evidence of her unwillingness to consummate their union, and that he would find a woman who would be a true and loving wife to him.

There was a lump in her throat as she paused, deciding to sign her baptismal name, forming the letters in a hand which trembled—'Isabella'. Quickly she added his name 'Rico' in firm letters at the top of the sheet, folded it and placed it in an envelope addressed to their room, with the securely packaged wedding and engagement rings he had given her, before handing it over to the receptionist.

Minutes later she was stepping into a taxi, her holdall in her hand, heading for the residential part of the city. Staring out at the crowded streets, the mêlée of casually dressed holidaymakers, she felt a twinge of apprehension. Resolutely she refused to dwell on it. The die was cast. It was too late for regrets.

Eventually she found a room in the old part of the town in a narrow street, darkened by the height of buildings. It was small, without air-conditioning, but it was clean and the windows opened out over a small street fruit market, the warm ripe scent of persimmons, mangoes, nesperas and pawpaw lingering long after the stalls had closed. It wasn't cheap, but she could afford it, and hopefully it wouldn't be long before she found work.

Wearily she sank down on the bed. When would Rico miss her? Surely in about two or three hours he would expect her to have returned? A query at the hairdressers' would elicit the fact that she'd never had an appointment; a visit to their room would find her letter . . . She shivered, imagining his face when he realised she'd gone. He didn't care for her, but his pride would be hurt, the powerful *machismo* that ruled his life damaged.

Stoically she prepared herself for the long wait before the sun set and she could begin her quest for a life of her own.

In the early hours of the evening she presented herself at A Cabana Laranja and asked to see the manager.

She'd dressed carefully for the occasion, wearing the scarlet dress that was Rico's favourite, letting her hair fall in a shining mass on to her shoulders.

'*Boa tarde*,' she greeted him with elegant assurance, her Portuguese as fluent as her English. 'I'm Sable Guimares, the daughter of Laura Armstrong. Like my mother I'm a cabaret artiste—and I'm available for bookings.'

CHAPTER TEN

THE faintly rancid smell of greasepaint and cold cream clung to the murky atmosphere of the tiny room as Sable tried to bring some colour to her pale cheeks and some lustre to her tired eyes. The naked light bulb over the battered table was desperately unkind to her, strengthening the shadows under her eyes and throwing the lines of strain on her tense face into cruel relief.

Laying the powder brush down, she selected a carmine-red lipliner, blocking in its vibrant colour on her soft mouth. How much longer could she bear to work in these conditions? The tired image in the spotted mirror gave her no comfort.

Ten days had gone by before she'd even found a job. Ten days when she'd been forced to realise that none of the more reputable nightclubs were in the least bit interested in her or what she could do. Not even one audition, she thought bitterly, just polite amazement and amused incredulity that she'd even thought of approaching them.

So she'd searched farther afield until she'd found the Tejo Club. The money she was offered was abysmal, and, since she wasn't going to increase her income by entertaining the clients after the show as the other girls did, she wasn't even earning a living wage. The only thing to its credit was that she was getting valuable experience performing before a live audience. Not that the men who came and leered and shouted at her were discriminatory, just effusive. Still, she consoled herself with a heavy heart, it was better than nothing.

Her holiday money had been generous, but she'd had to buy her own make-up and stage costumes—a different one for each of the three spots she appeared in—and they hadn't been cheap! With the prospect of obtaining a really worthwhile booking a vague mirage on the horizon, she was having to eke out the balance of her finance most carefully.

The sound of catcalls and raucous cheering from outside was increasing. Sarita and Dorinda, the exotic dancers who preceded her act, must be reaching their finale. In a few minutes she'd be out there, on the raised podium, trying to placate an audience yelling for further stimulation.

A dash of crimson to the inner corner of each eye and she was ready, surveying her painted face with distaste. A deep shudder ran through her. What would her father or Rico think if they could see her like this—impact replacing art at the instructions of the manager? Angrily she brushed away a tear. When she'd walked out on her husband she'd effectively alienated herself from both of them. Jaime Guimares would never countenance such a step. And as for Rico, as far as he was concerned she would be dead . . .

Rising to her feet, she took a dispassionate survey of her costume—the tight-fitting gold lamé dress zipped to just about the knee, opening out into a fishtail for ease of walking—the stiletto-heeled shoes, the height of which threw every curve of her body into a provocative posture. Carefully she reached to the dressing-table, picking up the long, black, imitation silk gloves she needed, drawing them on and fastening two glittering rhinestone bracelets on her wrist.

There was a sound outside, a burst of laughter, and the two girls with whom she shared the dressing-room burst in.

'Good luck, sweetie.' The elder of the two pretty Mexican girls gave her a commiserating smile. 'I think you'll need it. They're baying for blood tonight.'

'Thanks.' Sable returned the smile. The two girls were the only friends she had now. 'I'll try to keep them happy.'

Standing out of sight as she was introduced, Sable touched the little gold *figa* that had been Toninho's gift. Every night since this ordeal had started, six nights ago, she'd worn it as a talisman—a tie with the past. A reminder of her wedding day to Rico whom she'd walked out on and whom, over the past days of disappointment and heartache she now realised, far too late, she loved. Yes, *loved*.

It was a dreadful irony that she'd had to run away from him before she'd realised the true depth of her feelings for him, and now her newly found knowledge was a misery that outweighed everything else. If only she'd been less vulnerable at the time of Ria's unexpected news, she could surely have coped with it better, but she'd allowed her outrage and hurt to blind her to her true feelings.

Impossible to say exactly when Rico had stolen her heart. She had tried to build up a wall of indifference to him ever since his dramatic début into her life, and for a while she had managed to deceive herself, clinging on to the memory of Simon, unwilling to admit that her father had judged him so accurately. When Simon's letter had destroyed the last illusion she had cherished about him, she had been freed to recognise just how much she cared for the handsome Brazilian who teased and tormented her but whose presence in her life had given it an added dimension.

She had loved him when she had accepted his unexpected proposal of marriage, although her brain had been slow in admitting what her heart was telling it. She had hoped, oh, so desperately, that he loved her too, that the physical rapport between them was a manifestation of that. She had dared to believe he did . . . and then she had learned the truth . . .

She had told herself she hated him; almost come to believe it. It had taken these days of absence from him to recognise just how badly she had been fooling herself. Now it was too late. Not that she had had any real choice. Loving him or not, it would have been impossible to live with him as his wife, enduring his lovemaking, bearing his children, knowing all the time that he had chosen her for the role only because she was his godfather's kin!

Stifling her tears, she heard her stage name announced—'The Tejo Club are proud to announce the beautiful, talented singer from across the Atlantic—Laurita!' Her music started and she was walking on to the small stage, smiling like the professional she'd wanted to be, commencing her opening number, projecting her melodious voice above the noise surrounding her.

Her first song had a simple theme. She was not, she informed the audience, in the market for love. If any man thought he could buy her favours with gifts, then he was in for a disappointment. Only love could win her—only love. The words were so close to her own heart that she wouldn't have been able to sing a note without bursting into tears if she hadn't brought her professionalism to bear on her performance. As it was, she managed to distance herself from both her own emotions and the audience, standing in the spotlight singing the words first in Portuguese and then, for the benefit of the tourists, in English.

Suddenly there was a movement in the crowd. Even in

the darkness Sable felt the ripple of violence part them
as a man forced his way to the front. It wasn't unusual
for a member of the audience to try to fondle a female
performer, and it was something she lived in dread of
happening to her.

Backing away, her hand seizing the microphone from
its stand and holding it in front her like a weapon, her
heart thundering with fear, she only knew the intruder
was dressed totally in black and that he was making
directly for her. Only when he entered the circle of light
that surrounded her did she recognise Rico. A
terrifyingly transformed Rico, dark-browed and thin-
lipped, his eyes burning with a black anger that
transfixed her to the spot.

'Don't . . .' She tried to fend him off, panicking at the
evidence of revenge that turned his face into a cold,
hard mask. Then the microphone had been torn from
her shaking grasp to clatter on the floor and she was
being lifted, fireman-style, over his shoulder, and
carried out into the night air, leaving behind a wildly
cheering audience.

'Stay where you are—don't move.' He deposited her
on the pavement with such determination that her ankle
gave and she had to steady herself on his arm before he
flung her hand away from him. 'I'm going to get a taxi,'
he told her, brilliant black eyes daring her to defy him.
'And if you move so much as one step, I'll give you the
thrashing you so desperately deserve, here and now.'
His cold appraisal followed the trembling lines of her
body in the figure-fitting dress. 'And I guarantee there
isn't a man in this city who would come to your aid in
the circumstances!'

Sable stood motionless where he'd left her as he
strode to the nearby road junction, stepping off the
pavement and hailing a cruising cab. It would be

impossible to move even if she'd wanted to. Her whole body felt boneless, on the point of collapse.

'Here . . .' He opened the car door, taking her arm and thrusting her into the back seat, climbing in beside her, directing the driver to the hotel where they'd stayed.

So he hadn't gone back to his ranch as she'd supposed. She'd underestimated his desire for vengeance. Because that was what had kept him in Rio. If she'd ever doubted it, then one look at his grim face was enough to assure her that it wasn't a reconciliation he had on his mind.

She leaned back against the soft upholstery, closing her eyes, praying she'd be given the strength to suffer his retribution with dignity. However hard he struck her, nothing could equal the pain of loving him and knowing she could never tell him so.

At the hotel, he paid off the taxi and turned his glowering gaze on her.

'Are you going to walk in or do I carry you?'

'I'll walk.' She lifted her head proudly, walking at his side, not daring to seek the support of his arm, ashamed of her garishly painted face and the image she must present. For one wild moment she wondered if she'd be refused admittance, hanging back as Rico collected their key, and keeping her eyes downcast as they entered the lift, aware of the curious looks thrown in her direction.

When Rico opened the door and stood back, commanding her to enter, she was braced to face his anger, but even so, his opening words astounded her.

'Finish it, Sable!' His voice was harsh, raw with emotion.

'Finish?' She flinched from the censure of his gaze. 'Finish—what?'

'Your act. Your striptease. What else?' His white

teeth gleamed in a humourless smile and she could see a
heavy pulse beating in his throat where the 'V' of his black
shirt parted. 'You'll never have such an appreciative
audience as you have now—so, go on—strip!'

She stared at him in horror. 'It was a song, not a
striptease! For God's sake, Rico, it was a *song!*'

She stared at him, horror darkening her eyes as she
saw he didn't believe her.

'Why are you waiting?' he queried coldly. 'Is it music
you want?' Five steps and he'd reached the Musac
fitment by the bed, and pressed it into life. Warm,
passionate Latin American music flooded the room.
'Ideal,' he gave his verdict succinctly.

'Rico, for pity's sake . . . I can't!' she implored him,
willing him to save her from such a cold-blooded
degradation.

'Do you think I don't know what those clubs are
like?' His voice was harsh with fury. 'I've visited
enough these past days in my search for you. Oh, you've
got a pretty enough little voice, my dear, but nothing
will persuade me that it was enough by itself to get you
work!'

A deep wave of colour suffused her face as Sable
silently acknowledged the validity of his acid remark.
She *had* been asked to strip by the manager, and she had
resolutely refused to do so. To her surprise, he had
accepted her decision, adding cynically, 'Perhaps when
you're a little hungrier, darling, you may change your
tune!'

She would never be that hungry! she had told herself.
Besides, she had every intention of leaving the Tejo the
moment she could find somewhere less sordid.

Rico's scowl deepened as her blush seemed to confirm
his worst conclusions.

'The sooner you start, the sooner it will be finished,'

he told her unremittingly, his eyes burning her with contempt. 'If you can do it in a room full of strangers, you can do it for me—your husband.' He was merciless in his resolve.

'Rico, please, I'm sorry . . .' She wouldn't weep in front of him. 'I shouldn't have run away like I did, I deserve your anger. If you're going to beat me, then I won't try and stop you, but you must believe me . . .'

'Beat you?' Dark eyebrows winged in mocking amazement. 'Whatever you may deserve, and whatever I threatened you with earlier, be assured I don't beat women or horses. It bruises their tender flesh and breaks their spirits. Why should I wish to destroy what pleases me, hmm?'

She sought for any sign of compassion on his handsome face—and found none, only a clinical appraisal that told her he would spend the rest of the night waiting for her obedience, if necessary.

If she'd hated him it would have been painful. Loving him, it was agony—a denial of love and tenderness in the cold self-interests of sex. For that was obviously his interest, his only interest in her now. But then, what was different? Hadn't that always been the case? Only now there was an element of revenge in what he intended to do with her, and she wasn't sure she could survive whatever cruelty he had planned at her expense.

Ashen-faced, she sought his taut face for any sign of softness and, finding none, began to do as he instructed. Unclipping the bracelets, she peeled off the long silken gloves beneath his contemptuous scrutiny. Fingers functioning stiffly, she stooped to the fastener of the reversed zip, pulling it open as she rose until the whole dress parted at her breasts. Coyness would be even more demeaning. She let the dress fall to the ground.

She barely heard his harsh exhalation of breath as she

stood revealed in a brief flesh-coloured body-shaper, her feet encased in scarlet sandals at the end of each bare golden leg.

'Give me your foot.'

She obeyed the hoarse command, as Rico sat down on the bed. Supporting herself with one hand against the wall, she watched with a growing tension as he bent over his self-imposed task of undoing the strap.

'And the other.'

The second sandal joined the first on the floor.

'And now you can finish the rest yourself.'

She wasn't misled by the softness of the instruction, as the throbbing rhythm of the music pulsed in the background. The hard glitter in Rico's eyes as he lounged back, watching her every move, told her everything she had to know. Confirming what she'd dreaded from the moment they'd entered the room.

Catching her lower lip between her teeth, her raven hair falling towards her breasts as she lowered her head in shame, Sable pushed the simple garment towards the floor.

With one swift movement Rico came to her, gathering her in his arms, running his palms down her naked body, capturing her mouth with an ardent passion that was shocking in its intensity. As the warmth of their mouths merged Sable felt her pulse quicken and a tingling awareness in her loins begin to spread warm tentacles of desire through the rest of her body.

This was the man she loved, the man whose arms she'd craved to lie in time and again over the past days. Even now, when he was treating her like some *rapariga* he'd bought for a night's pleasure, it was impossible to stop her response. Her fingers lifted to thread through the black crown of lustrous hair that capped his well-shaped head.

'Isabella—*minha* Isabella . . .' It was a throaty whisper as his response matched and overtook her own.

Mesmerised by his nearness, intoxicated by the scent and taste of him, Sable pressed herself against him, unbearably excited by the touch of fabric against her bare flesh, she felt the male hardness of his body hunt against her for fulfilment, before he drew back from her, uttering a soft laugh.

'That was a very amateur performance, *meu amor*. I shall have to teach you how to improve it when we return to Ribatejo . . .' he informed her huskily. 'But then there are many things you will have to learn, and what better time for your first lesson than now?'

The soft question was faintly menacing as with a sudden purpose Rico pushed her away from him, his eyes making an impertinent study of her naked form. She took the opportunity of gathering up her abandoned dress, holding it against her as she backed away like a wounded animal, hurt by the cynical twist of his sensuous mouth.

'Oh, no, you don't. Not this time, *meu amor*!' The slight tremble of his deep tones told her that, despite the cat and mouse game he appeared to be playing with her, Rico was already enthralled in the net of desire as he walked towards her. The flush across his cheekbones, the devilish sparkle in his deep-set eyes warned her that this time he meant to have his own way, and she cowered against the door, anchoring herself to its protection by seizing the handle with her free hand. 'This isn't the time for living out virginal fantasies, since both of us know that it's a long time since you could lay claim to that unsullied state,' he told her harshly, reaching out a demanding hand towards her, as she gasped her consternation.

'Don't bother to lie, *minha mulher*. I married you

with my eyes wide open. When your father wrote to me, he told me he could no longer hope for a marriage between us since you were not a virgin.' He stared down into her horrified face. 'Perhaps he guessed I wasn't to be so easily dissuaded and felt it was his duty as a gentleman to give me such information.' She gasped at the cruel beauty of his cold face. 'You see, it's not unknown in this country for a wife to be killed on her wedding night by a husband who finds his rights have already been pre-empted!'

Sable felt the blood drain from her face, as the words to justify herself refused to come to her tongue.

'And how many others have there been besides Simon, hmm?' She wasn't deceived by the gentleness of the question. Within Rico's hard-fleshed body a raging fire was mounting, fed by emotions she could only guess at. 'Why defend the citadel when one man has already breached the gate, eh? Do you have an appetite for "love", my dark beauty? When I hold you in my arms and feel your response, I believe you do . . .'

His hand, moving with devastating speed, seized the dress behind which she sheltered, tearing it from her grasp and leaving her defenceless to his searching stare.

'It's not true . . .' Aware he was hardly listening to her, Sable repeated the words again. 'Rico, I swear it, it's not true . . . nothing's true . . .'

'Is it payment you want?' Black eyes bored into her as he continued, seemingly oblivious of her interruption. 'Don't lie to me, Sable. I told you, I know the kind of club you were working at. The only possible way you could make a living was by selling your body to the clients on the side.' Strong hands grasped her shoulders, drawing her away from the door with an irrefutable power.

'How many lovers have you had these last two weeks?

Three, four—one a night? How did they pay you—in *cruzado* notes stuffed beneath your pillow, or with gold like this . . .' Before she could make a move to stop him, he caught the thin chain round her neck, breaking it with a sharp twist and throwing the *figa* over his shoulder with a snort of disgust.

'Stop it—stop it!' It was almost a scream as she saw the small gold charm sink into the pile of the carpet.

'Not this time,' came the taut reply. 'This time your luck has left you. Whether you like it or not, your uncle entrusted you to my keeping the day he agreed to our wedding at your request. The time has come to teach you that love is not a prerequisite of sexual enjoyment, and I mean to ensure it's a lesson you'll never forget!'

Not like this—oh, not like this. Sable bit back her pleas, knowing the time for mercy was past, as Riço lifted her in his arms and tossed her on to the bed.

Pausing only to wrench off his shirt, he lowered himself along the length of her, contemplating her ashen face with narrowed eyes. 'Did you really think I'd let you run away from me?' He framed her face with the palms of his hands. 'Haven't I paid a high enough price for you—marriage, a share in my ranch, a stake in my future? What more do you want from me?'

Love, trust, tenderness, affection. She could only say the words in her mind, closing her eyes to shut away the sight of his beloved face and what she could read on it. Now, when she needed him so desperately, she had lost him so utterly . . .

'Sable . . .' She felt his mouth on her cheek, knew it to be trailing down her neck, caressing her aching breasts, whispering with impossible softness across their inflamed peaks. 'It doesn't have to be this way. I don't have to take. You could give . . .'

'Do what you must.' Her heart breaking, Sable could

no longer prevent the slow, sad tears of desolation from running down her cheeks. 'I have nothing to give you.' Nothing except my undying love, a gift you would regard with contempt . . . The unspoken words echoed in the barren emptiness of her mind.

Expecting to be taken at her word, when she felt Rico move from her side she assumed he was going to remove the rest of his clothes. Minutes later she felt the soft chiffon of her nightdress fall across her exposed body.

'Put it on, Sable.' He sounded inestimably weary. 'Tomorrow we make an early start for Ribatejo. I've been away far too long. There are many arrangements for the future to be made, and nothing can be done until your father had been located and informed of our marriage and our wish to terminate it. In the meantime you will come with me to the ranch and reside there as my nominal wife.'

'You're going to apply to have the marriage voided?' she whispered.

Two weeks ago and she would have greeted the news with triumph. Now, although it was the only logical answer, it struck her like a death knell.

'That's what you want, isn't it?' he asked bleakly. 'Yes, I'm finally persuaded it was the biggest mistake I've ever made and there's nothing to be gained from trying to rectify it. It seems we're too far apart ever to reconcile our differences.'

'I must make some phone calls before we leave.'

Dressed in a light suit and dark brown open-necked shirt, Rico was elegant and controlled—a mile away from the tight-lipped man who'd waited only to pull his shirt on again after his harsh declaration, before striding from the bedroom in the early hours of the same morning, leaving Sable to face the remaining hours before dawn alone.

She'd no idea where he'd gone, only that Rio had plenty of opportunities for a man seeking female consolation if that had been his aim.

When she'd awakened from a sleep tortured by nightmares, he'd already returned, showered and dressed, and was in the process of packing.

Over a traditional Brazilian breakfast of milky coffee and buttered rolls served in their room, Sable had followed his lead in communication. It appeared that the relationship between them was to be one of polite indifference. Instead of the further recriminations she'd anticipated, Rico treated her as if she was a distant acquaintance. His manners were faultless . . . and caused her as much pain as if he'd continued to act the outraged husband.

Finishing her own packing, she listened with desultory interest as he contacted Ribatejo, informing the ranch manager of their imminent arrival and requesting a car to meet them at Porto Alegre. Several more calls followed, obviously of a business nature, as Sable watched him, letting her gaze wander over the broad shoulders, the lean waist, tight hips and long, muscular legs clothed by an expert tailor to emphasise their strength and grace. She swallowed deeply, trying to control the flood of longing that surged through her, making her pulse race and her breathing uneven.

As if sensing her rapt attention Rico turned suddenly, dark eyes narrowing, pinioning her white, strained face with his derisive gaze.

Unable to bear his cold scrutiny, she scrambled to her feet, making for the bathroom to repair her make-up. If she couldn't force a smile to her lips then she'd paint one on, she lectured herself sternly. The Guimares had pride, and she owed it to her own self-esteem not to betray the desolation she felt.

Late afternoon the same day, seated in the back of a chauffeur-driven car at Rico's side, she pondered on the upheaval she was about to cause in his life. For six years he'd devoted himself to improving the ranch, at the expense of his social life. Now, at the age of thirty, he wanted the wife and children who would turn the estate into a home.

She thought of Vitor and Ria and their two babies, glancing sideways at the man beside her. He was leaning back, his eyes closed, the proud profile relaxed. Did he envy them their secure happiness? Had he wanted a woman to love or had he sought only to satisfy his body's needs and the duties of his heritage.

Whatever the answer, he would have a long wait ahead of him before he could achieve it. The dissolution of their marriage was bound to be messy and protracted.

Sighing deeply, Sable placed her hand on the lean thigh beside her own in an automatic gesture of compassion.

'What's wrong? Are you unwell?' Her touch had been feather-light, yet enough to disturb Rico, causing his thickly lashed eyes to open and regard her with a measure of concern.

Quickly she withdrew her hand. 'I just wondered how much further it is now.'

'We've been on the estate for the past half-hour,' he informed her curtly. 'We'll reach the house in another ten minutes.' He paused, before adding coolly, 'The news of my marriage caused great excitement among the staff at the ranch. There's bound to be a welcoming committee. It would be discourteous to spoil their pleasure at your arrival, so I would appreciate your co-operation in playing the part of the blushing bride for the next hour or so. With your acting experience, I fancy that shouldn't present too much difficulty?'

He would never know just how difficult it was! She inclined her head gracefully. 'Naturally, I wouldn't want to spoil your homecoming.' And had to be content with the small grunt that greeted her assurance.

Just over an hour later, having dealt graciously with the effusive greetings of the household staff assembled in the wide hallway to welcome her, she found herself being ushered over the threshold of a large room on the upper floor of the rambling two-floor building.

'This is the master bedroom, but don't be disturbed, I shan't be sharing it with you.' Rico walked away towards the facing wall of inbuilt cupboards without a glance in her direction, allowing Sable to make quick appraisal of her surroundings.

Yet once more a bridal bed awaited her. This time it was an enormous four-poster, dressed overall in shades of oatmeal and pale blue, dominating the spacious room which had obviously been prepared with loving hands, from the vase of flowers on a small table to the bowl of fruit beside the bed.

'You're having another room made up for you?' she asked in a small voice.

'No, that won't be necessary.' He turned from surveying a cupboard amply stocked with male wearing-apparel. 'I've been away much too long as it is. There are problems which need my personal attention and I don't mean to keep them waiting any longer.'

'You mean you're not staying here?' Her voice shook. It was bad enough that he hated her, but she'd hoped to spend a few more days in his company, enjoying the sweet agony that just looking at him gave her, before he took steps to end their turbulent marriage. Now it seemed even that was lost to her.

'There's no need for alarm.' Dark eyes dwelt on her pale face. 'Nothing will be required of you. I've instructed the staff to treat you as an honoured guest until I return. The house and the stables are entirely at your disposal, provided you accept the advice of the grooms as to which horse you ride, and are escorted at all times.'

'I'm a good horsewoman!' she boasted proudly, then bit her lip, wishing she'd stayed silent as Rico's riposte taunted her.

'So you told me once before. But the grounds of Ribatejo are extensive, and I have already wasted too much time in chasing after you,' she was informed drily.

Reminded of her irresponsible departure from the hotel in Rio, Sable turned away, avoiding the censure of those magnetic eyes. At the time she had seen no other way . . . If only she had known then what she did now . . .

To relieve her tension, she pulled the restraining pins from her upswept hair, shaking it free and allowing it to fall in a tumbling mass to the shoulders of the white linen suit she was wearing in deference to the cooler climate of the south.

'Will you be away long?' It was little more than a whisper as she tried to hide her terrible sense of loss.

His lips twisted. 'A week, ten days . . . Is that long enough to restore your peace of mind, *meu amor*?'

Flinching at the sarcasm of the endearment, Sable watched him begin to gather clothes from the cupboard.

'How will you travel—by jeep?' she asked hopefully.

'Indeed not.' He turned raised eyebrows to confront her. 'I shall travel the way *gauchos* have always travelled this land—by horse.'

'But, Rico . . .' His laconic responses were torturing her. 'It would surely be much faster by jeep, and you've had no sleep. Couldn't you rest a while first if you changed your mind and took motorised transport?'

Broad shoulders shrugged with careless nonchalance. 'I rested on the plane, and my need for sleep has never been great. As for speed—believe me, I find it more satisfying to feel real horsepower between my thighs than any mechanical equivalent.'

'But you'll have dinner first?' The deep need she had to delay his departure from her even by minutes drove her onward.

'I take my own food with me.' He dismissed her suggestion with scant regard. 'And now, if you'll excuse me, I mean to have a bath before I leave.' Dark eyes gleamed with mocking malice. 'It will be the last one for several days, so I mean to make the most of it.' His pensive glance encompassed the bed. 'If you're tired, you could have a sleep before dinner.' He consulted his watch. 'You have two hours. Otherwise . . .' he'd seen the slight shake of her head, 'I suggest you go downstairs, where you'll find Lucia, the housekeeper waiting to show you around your new domain and receive your instructions.'

It was as clear a dismissal as she'd ever had. Sable turned and started for the door.

'Just one more thing . . .' Rico's head appeared from behind the door leading to the bathroom. 'If it's your status with the servants that's worrying you, be at the stables in an hour's time to wish me *até logo!*'

He didn't wait for her response, closing the door with a thud as he disappeared behind it.

It was just after an hour when Sable, having faithfully followed the instructions she'd been given, arrived in the stable yard, to a scene of great activity, most of it centering round a fiery-looking stallion, its ebony coat sleek and shining beneath the working stock saddle which had replaced the more customary Western-style saddle, a sure

sign that Rico's activities were going to be active rather
than supervisory.

'*Senhora* . . .' One of the stablehands approached her
with a diffident smile. 'The *senhor* will be leaving in a
minute. He's just giving a few last-minute instructions.'

Hardly had he finished speaking than Rico strode out
of one of the buildings. Sable felt her mouth grow dry as
every nerve-end in her body prickled with a curious
anticipation. She'd never seen him like this before.
Gone was the suave landowner. In his place was a
gaucho dressed in the accepted garb of the *pampas*. A
red checked shirt with rolled-up sleeves fitted snugly
across his wide shoulders, the neck open, revealing a
scarlet neck-scarf. A broad-brimmed black hat was
tipped over his forehead at a rakish angle. Only the
close-fitting black trousers tucked into the calf-high
leather boots were a break with tradition.

'Isabella—*meu amor*.' He came towards her, a rolled-
up cape under one arm, a stock whip looped in the other
hand. Only she was close enough to see the ironic glitter
in his black eyes as he reached her.

Immediately one of the stablehands came forward,
taking the cape and whip from his imperious hands.

'Is everything in order?' Rico's tone was clipped as he
addressed the man.

'*Sim, senhor*—everything. Food, water, lassoes,
knives and the short-wave radio. Everything is packed.'

'Good!' He bit the word out tersely before turning to
draw Sable into his arms. '*Minha querida*,' he drawled.
'How much it pains me to leave you like this. How
urgently I look for our reunion.'

'Rico—don't . . .' she whispered, unbearably hurt by
the cruelty of his pretence.

'But we must save your face, sweet Sable. For the
next few days you must command these people's respect

as mistress of the Rancho Ribatejo. We must show them you have my confidence—and my love, must we not?'

Before she could object again, he seized her small, defiant chin in one hand, raising her face and lowering his own, taking possession of her mouth with a brutal passion that left her gasping for breath, her senses reeling from the clean, tangy man-scent of him, her knees buckling from the power of his embrace.

'*Até logo, minha mulher* . . .' He swung himself up into the saddle of the waiting horse with lissom grace, gathering the reins loosely in one hand. Mounted long-stirruped, he urged the animal to motion with a nudge of his heels as the men in the yard moved aside to allow him exit.

'*Até logo, meu marido* . . .' Sable played her part out to the last speech, before turning away, her eyes scalding with bitter tears.

Only she of all the people there knew she shouldn't have used the phrase 'goodbye until the next time'. She should have said *adeus*. The word of final parting, because Rico was lost to her as completely as if he'd indeed been the phantom cowboy she'd first supposed him to be, riding away into the distance to seek the love which always escaped him, leaving only the burning brand of his lips on her own as the sole reminder that he had once desired her.

CHAPTER ELEVEN

As SABLE rode into the yard astride the chestnut mare which had become her regular mount, the black stallion already there swished his long tail and snorted, tossing his flowing mane as if in greeting.

Rico was back! A thrill of excitement surged through her as she swung one heavy-denim-covered leg across the back of her mount and dropped lightly to the ground.

For nine days she'd been existing in the vacuum caused by his absence. Nine long, lonely days when her only solace had been the feel of the wind in her untamed hair and the sun on her face as she'd tested the speed and stamina of the beautiful mare entrusted to her care, riding over the rolling plains, experiencing for herself the powerful magnetism they could exercise over those who loved them.

Leaving her mount to the care of the groom who'd been following her at a respectful distance, she approached the man who was grooming Rico's stallion.

'Senhor de Braganza has returned, *nao*?' Her heart was beating so fast, that the question came out in a breathless rush.

'*Sim, Senhora* . . . two hours ago.' The man's smile followed her as she turned away.

Two hours! Where would he be now? She forced herself to walk sedately towards the house, her mind in a turmoil. Dear heavens, how she'd longed for this moment—wanting nothing more than to feast her eyes on him, to savour his presence. Beside her intensity of feeling for Rico, every other emotion she'd ever harboured paled into insignificance. How could she have ever imagined she'd loved the selfish, vain, avaricious Simon Layton?

'Sable? Ah, I thought I recognised your tread.'

She'd started walking through the wide entrance-hall, immersed in her thoughts, and suddenly Rico was there in front of her, barring her way, the door of the small room he used as an office flung open.

For a moment words eluded her as she drank in every detail of his appearance. Still dressed in typical *gaucho* style, it was clear he'd bathed and changed. Her hungry eyes registered the pristine crispness of the blue checked shirt, the newness of the tight black trousers, the freshly cleaned leather boots, before returning to linger on his face.

The deepened tan couldn't hide the harshness of his cheekbones or mask the lines of strain that bisected each lean cheek. It could only add lustre to the dark eyes behind their protective furl of jet lashes, and give deeper contrast to his perfect teeth as the beautiful, faintly cruel mouth twisted into a smile. His hair was longer too, curling damply across the top of his ears, clustering on the tender nape of his neck.

'I've only just learned you were back. I've been out riding.' Her own voice sounded strained, or perhaps it was the pounding blood in her ears that clouded her judgement.

'So I see.' A glimmer of amusement softened his tone.

For the first time, Sable realised her own appraisal was being returned with interest. Oh, why hadn't he given her a chance to change before subjecting her to such an intense scrutiny? Despairingly aware of the way her white silk blouse was clinging to her damp skin and the total dishevelment of her untamed hair, she raised one hand to comb trembling fingers through its wayward tresses.

'I have to go and have a shower.' She tried to move forward but was waylaid.

'Later. Now it's important that I speak to you. I have very good news for you. Excellent news, in fact.' He stood aside, motioning her to precede him into the room.

Sable stared at him, her heart sinking as she took the chair he indicated. Somehow he'd brought about the annulment of their marriage without further formality! It had to be that. What other news would give him such a complacent air of satisfaction? Even though he'd been out on the range, he'd been in radio contact with the office. With Rico, anything was possible!

'It's about your father.' He took up a stance in front of her, thumbs hooked in his trouser pockets, lean, tanned fingers spread on his thighs.

'You've managed to locate him at last!' She leaned forward eagerly.

'Yes, indeed.' He hesitated. 'Sable . . . I don't think you were ever aware of the fact, but recently he's been far from well.'

'Papa?' She felt herself blanch. 'No, I never guessed.' Her eyes beseeched him to confirm that the news he had was as good as he'd led her to believe, as an icy band seemed to squeeze her heart.

'Why should you?' Rico shrugged. 'He did his best to hide it from you. But a few months ago he had to face the fact that unless he underwent open-heart surgery his days were numbered.'

'*Mai de Deus* . . .' The words were a pathetic prayer as she rose to her feet in distress, shock mirrored in her widened eyes.

'It's all right!' Rico came to her, holding her upper arms, supporting her as a wave of dizziness made her knees buckle. 'The operation is over and done. They bypassed the obstruction causing the problem and he's made a total recovery. His surgeon couldn't be more pleased. I was waiting for the final clearance and his permission before I told you, and when I learned on the radio yesterday morning that it had come through, I returned immediately.'

'That's why no one could reach him . . .' Her agile mind leaped to the solution. 'But *you* knew what was happening . . . all the time!' She clung to Rico's shoulders, gripping them hard in her agony. 'And Uncle Roberto . . . he must have known as well. But what about me? Why didn't he tell *me*?' Deep pain reflected in the sapphire blue of her eyes. 'I should have been there with him! Oh, God, Rico, why did he send me away? Did he despise me so much?'

'Hush, *meu amor*.' She felt his hand stroke her hair as if he were soothing a child. 'It was because he *loved* you that he sent you here. If the operation had failed, he wanted you to be with your family—people who would love and cherish you, help you to cope with the formalities.'

'I should have been with him!' Fire flashed in her eyes as she made the passionate declaration. 'And if things hadn't worked out I would have been able to cope by myself. Thousands of other women have to, and I'm as strong and capable as they are.'

'I don't doubt it.' Gently Rico loosened her tight grip, retaining a hold on her trembling hands. 'But your father's Brazilian and he follows the code he was raised with. Women are to be protected in our society, sheltered wherever possible from the harshness of life. It's more than a man's duty, Sable, to protect the women in his care, it's his pleasure and purpose in life. If he defaults, then his honour and dignity become victims of that failure. Your father was sure he was doing the right thing.'

Tears misted Sable's eyes as she slumped down in the chair again. Now she could see things clearly. From the moment of diagnosis her father had always intended for her to visit Uncle Roberto. Her involvement with Simon must have appalled him, and having satisfied himself that the young actor had nothing to offer her, he'd turned the circumstances to his advantage, hiding the real purpose behind her enforced holiday.

But Rico was continuing to speak, with the air of a man unburdening himself. 'Even his plans for the two of us were based on nothing but a genuine affection for both of us and a certainty that we were made for each other!' He gave a short, grim laugh. 'When he came to my father's funeral, and showed me your photograph I must admit I was inclined to agree with him, and the idea of having a fiancée being groomed and prepared for him the other side of the Atlantic was an amusing thought for the hubristic young man I was then.' His eyes lingered thoughtfully on her upturned face. 'As the years went by he kept me informed of your progress, first at school, then at college. He'd always said he would introduce you to the idea when you were ready for it, but somehow that day didn't arrive until it was too late, did it?'

'No,' she murmured sadly.

Rico shook his head resignedly. 'Then a couple of months ago he wrote to me saying that not only had you refused to consider meeting me—even before he'd had a chance to tell you my name or who I was—but that you'd made an unfortunate alliance, and since you had lost your virginity to this scoundrel, you were clearly unsuitable to be my wife.'

'Rico, for pity's sake . . .' Sable half rose in the chair, distress draining every remnant of colour from her face.

'No!' He commanded her silence. 'Hear me out, Sable. It's the least I owe you, and I want to prove to you that your father's innocent of collusion: that he has never stopped loving you or wanting you to be happy. All the fault for what's happened between us lies with me—and me alone.'

She watched mutely as he moved away, walking towards the window before turning and swallowing deeply. 'I felt cheated and absolutely furious. Angry with you because you'd distressed your father when he was so ill, and because you'd shattered the dream I'd allowed myself to believe in.' His dark eyes seemed to bore right into her soul. 'I made up my mind I wouldn't be so easily dismissed. Jaime had told me he was sending you to stay with your uncle and I decided then and there that I'd find some pretext of meeting you, seeing what you were really like. I suppose I hoped I'd find that my paragon of virtue who had developed such clay feet wasn't nearly as beautiful or desirable as her photographs, and I could count myself lucky that she hadn't been foisted on me!'

He gave a bitter laugh as Sable glanced away, unable to bear the sight of his lips twisted in so cynical a smile. 'So I decided to mix business with "pleasure" and stay at the Granja Branca, which had the major advantage of being in the same district. Enquiries at the local Country Club elicited that both your uncle and cousin Luis were members, so I joined, planning to make their acquaintance, but it seems they were too busy escorting you around the sights to put in an appearance.'

'And then you met Aleixo?' Vaguely Sable was beginning to see the net that Fate had woven.

Rico nodded. 'A loquacious young man, only too keen to describe his infatuation with your pretty young cousin Rosina—so I cultivated his friendship, hoping he would lead me to you—instead . . .' His mouth tightened ominously. 'Believe me, I was appalled when he had that accident and confessed his plan to run off with her! The last thing I wanted was to see your family caught up in that kind of scandal. It would be no place for a stranger, and the more difficult it appeared the more determined I was to meet you socially!'

'So you never had any intention of kidnapping Rosina by proxy . . .' Light dawned in Sable's clouded mind.

'No, I came to send her back to her own bed with an admonition to behave herself.' The timbre of his voice had deepened. 'And found, instead of some silly teenager, that I was looking down at the face that had haunted my dreams for six years, the woman who, until her father had disillusioned me, was already my wife in my imagination!' He shrugged his shoulders. 'I lost my head.' A smile of self-mockery curved his strong mouth. 'In retrospect I can see how mixed my motives were—a desire to know you better, a wish to punish you by forcing you into an embarrassing position, a need to prove to myself that I couldn't be so summarily dismissed from your life . . .'

'Please—it doesn't matter now . . .' Every word he'd uttered had stung her like a hornet's bite. Even the relief she felt at knowing her father had not gone behind her back did nothing to salve the pain of Rico's contempt.

'It does matter, Sable!' he corrected her harshly. 'It matters to me that you know the truth before we part.' Relentlessly his hard voice continued. 'Our mock betrothal gave me all the opportunity I needed to be in your company, to get you out of my system. I told myself you were spoiled and wilful . . . you'd had at least one lover, perhaps more . . . you were hell-bent on following the same kind of career that had wrecked your father's marriage . . . that there was no way you could ever have been a suitable mistress for Ribatejo . . .'

'Then why did you ask me to marry you?' Sable's battered spirit rose from the hammering it had received as the ache round her heart became impossible to contain.

The sudden silence between them seemed a tangible entity. Sable could feel the heavy drag of her heartbeats, and there was a painful tightness in her chest, making it difficult for her to breathe, as she waited for his answer.

'You're a very beautiful woman, Sable.' His dark eyes devoured her unsmilingly. 'It was only natural that I should find you attractive. I even told myself I was acting in my godfather's interests. If I could encourage you to flirt with me, you might realise that there were other men in the world beside Simon Layton . . . But things rapidly got out of hand.'

Sable forced herself to hold his gaze. 'I see.'

'Do you?' He stared into her tightly controlled face. 'Do you see how deeply I fell into my own trap? That day on the golf course when you responded to me so sweetly and so passionately I realised I was no longer in control of the situation.' He exhaled a deep breath. 'And suddenly it didn't matter to me how many other lovers you had known; I knew I should have no peace until I became one of them.'

A cold shiver ran up Sable's spine as she marvelled at his intensity, shaking her head slightly as if in disbelief.

'Oh, it's true, *meu amor*,' he assured her bitterly. 'I told myself your favours were freely given, you were born to a less moral code than ours, that with a little encouragement I could make you forget Simon Layton entirely . . . Only one thing stopped me—Jaime Guimares was my godfather and that made you sacrosanct. The only way I could have you was in marriage.'

'And when Simon wrote me that letter you saw the perfect opportunity,' she said tonelessly.

'Yes.' He nodded. 'Don't think my conscience didn't trouble me the day we made our vows. I tried to persuade myself that you'd come to me voluntarily, that you'd never really loved Simon, but I knew I'd pressurised you by choosing the moment I did to propose. Even your aunt's unexpected appearance had worked in my favour.' He paused slightly before adding heavily, 'Oh, yes. On my wedding day I felt guilty as hell, and the last thing I was prepared to handle was your discovering I was Jaime's godson, and drawing all the wrong conclusions! I'd planned to break that news to you after our honeymoon, by which time I'd fooled myself into believing you would have welcomed it.' He made a weary gesture with one lean-fingered hand. 'Then, before I could even begin to explain, you dropped your own bombshell . . . You told me you were still in love with Simon.'

It had been her only protection against the explosion that had shattered her barely formulated dreams: a lie that had protected the last modicum of pride she had left. Now there was no point in denying it. She stared down at her hands clasped tightly in her lap. 'We married for all the wrong reasons . . .'

'Yes . . . and the blame for that was mine.' Rico swallowed painfully. 'If it's any consolation to you, I shall never forgive myself for forcing you into the kind of life you had to embrace to escape me . . . or for what I made you suffer before I came to my senses and realised there would never be a future for us together.

Neither do I have the audacity to beg for your foregiveness.' Humility sat strangely on his hard-boned face as he turned away from her, his hand reaching for the drawer of the nearby desk. 'Here . . . I had no right to take this from you. See, I've had it mended.'

Sable found herself staring down at the little golden fist she'd last seen disappearing into the carpet pile of the hotel in Rio. There'd been so much on her mind that she'd never even searched for it. A surge of courage streamed through her. At least now they were talking rationally she could put that part of the record straight!

'Thank you.' She took the offering, slipping it into her own pocket. 'I would have hated to lose it; my cousin Toninho gave it to me as a talisman on our wedding day.' She spoke coolly, seeing with pleasure the gaurded look of surprise on Rico's dark face. 'And I wouldn't want you to blame yourself too much for my adventures in Rio—not only were they instructive, but they were totally financed by my father. He'd sent me well equipped with travellers' cheques.'

'Is this true, Sable?' A sudden fire flashed in Rico's eyes as roughly he challenged her. 'Or is it a final act of compassion to try and ease the agony of my conscience before you go from my life for ever?'

It was an effort to control the wild thudding of her heart as she lifted her shoulders dismissively. 'Your conscience is your own affair, Rico. I certainly wouldn't lie to salve it. I promise you I am as innocent now as the day I came to Brazil.' She smiled ironically. He would never know just how innocent that was!

'Dear God, Sable. I don't deserve your charity . . .' His deep voice was strangely husky. 'If you only knew the torment I've been suffering, imagining what I'd forced you into facing . . . I haven't slept properly for days . . .'

'Rico—don't!' She was on her feet, holding his arms, staring up beseechingly into his face, her heart aching for him, seeing the evidence of that torment on his strained face. 'Believe me, you have nothing to regret. In fact I have to thank you. If I learned nothing else, I found out that I don't want to go on the stage after all . . . that I shall never be another Laura Armstrong . . .' She had reached out unconsciously for the kind of love that her mother had conjured from an audience only to find herself cheated yet again.

'I'm sorry.' Rico sounded as if he really meant it as he took her hands in his own. 'I'm sorry for everything that's happened between us. At least we have to be glad that your father has responded so well to treatment. I'm arranging for him to come here to Ribatejo to convalesce for a month or so. We shall have to choose our time carefully to tell him what we have done and how much we regret it.' He dropped her hands abruptly, as if touching her displeased him, and turned towards the door.

'Where are you going now?' Sable said the first thing that came to her mind, as his lean figure moved away from her.

'There's a celebration this evening over in the grounds of the estate houses. One of the *gauchos* has become a father for the first time. I have to show my face. It's expected of me, but there's no need for you to be present.' It seemed he had to make an effort to speak the terse sentences.

'But you're dining with me first?' How could she ask such a mundane question when her heart was breaking?

'There'll be plenty of food there.' A small, humourless smile played at the corners of his mouth. 'And don't be concerned, Sable. I've arranged for a spare room to be made ready for me.'

'Rico!' She called his name, her heart bursting with love for him, wanting to tell him, yet knowing she couldn't place this further burden on him. On the threshold he paused, one eyebrow lifted enquiringly. 'Nothing—only—I'm sorry, too. Sorry that I couldn't be what you wanted . . .' She turned away, feeling her throat tighten.

His harsh expletive brought her swinging round in amazement as he took two strides back into the room, seizing her by the shoulders, his fingers biting into her soft flesh.

'Dear God, Sable, don't tempt me any more! Don't you know yet that you are the *only* woman I have ever wanted? That it was only my own stupid pride that stopped me from admitting it to myself from the beginning? That it took the shock of your running away from me to show me the truth—that not only did I desire you but that you'd taken my heart and my mind by storm?'

'Rico—what are you saying?' Wide-eyed, Sable stared at him.

His voice was so low she could barely hear it, his gaze holding hers, his face taut with barely leashed emotion. 'That whatever my early motives were, they were no longer valid, hadn't been for a long time, because I'd fallen in love with you.' He was breathing heavily and she could feel the tremors that made his body tremble. 'I told myself it was only my pride that was hurt when you swore you still loved Simon, but the truth was I was racked with jealousy, anger and hurt, but still convinced that if only I could take you in my arms, lie with you in my bed, love you as I wanted to, I could make you forget him!'

She wanted to speak but his words had stunned her, turned her world around. Dared she believe what she had heard him say? Plaintively her shadowed eyes begged him to reaffirm it. As if responding to her dumb plea, his gripping fingers released their hold, but she remained where she was, watching the agony on his face, while deep inside her a tiny hope began to seed itself and grow.

'When you ran away from me, I could no longer fool myself. I knew I loved you. Not just for your beauty, but everything about you—your spirit, your sense of fun, your bright imagination and your lively mind. I swore an oath that if ever I found you again I would give you the freedom you had fought so desperately for.' His own mouth curved into a wry smile. 'But by the time I did, I'm afraid relief and fear and guilt had built into such a cyclone within me that I temporarily lost control of myself.'

'But you're going to have our marriage dissolved?' She managed to whisper, scarcely daring to believe what she had heard. 'That is what you still intend, isn't it?'

'Yes, Sable.' The dark head nodded assent. 'I realise now there's no other course. I love you far too much to hold you here against your will.'

Even while the words were circulating in her mind and she was trying to make sense of them, Rico was on his way from the room without a backwards glance at her stunned face. Before she could utter another sound he'd gone.

She was going mad! Sable held her aching head in both hands. Rico loved her, wanted her, yet he was sending her away . . . A fierce, tumultuous joy began to stream through her veins. Rico loved her! All she had to do was go to him and tell him she loved him too! Perhaps he would need a little persuading after all the stupid things she'd said and done, but dear heavens, she was prepared to spend the rest of her life persuading him if he really wanted her! But not like this. She glanced down at her coarse denims. First she would shower and change, and then she'd find him.

Even if she hadn't already known where the night's entertainment was being held, the flickering lights, the sound of music and the smell of roasting meat would have led her to it.

Making her way carefully on her spindly heels, the skirt of her scarlet dress swaying against the graceful movement of her hips, her hair cascading down her back, Sable looked every inch the gypsy that Rico had once called her.

'*Senhora!*' She'd reached the outskirts of the small crowd of estate workers to be enthusiastically greeted by the nearest group. 'We understood you were feeling unwell!'

'A slight headache. Gone without a trace.' She smiled cheerfully at them, the scarlet ear-rings dancing against the pale column of her neck. 'I wouldn't have missed this for anything. Now my husband has returned I hope to get to know all of you a lot better.' Appreciative smiles greeted her assurance as she added, 'Who's the lucky father?'

Eager hands guided her into the heart of the scene and introduced her to a bashful young man who received her congratulations with a delighted grin.

'You must eat, *senhora*!' A woman detached herself from the group, guiding her towards one of the several barbeques, drawing from its fiery surface a slender steel sword threaded with chunks of beef. 'This is *churrasco*.'

'Mmm, delicious!' Sable's sharp teeth bit into the juicy meat, but her exquisitely made-up eyes were not on the food, as systematically she searched the happy gathering for a sign of Rico.

'You must drink to the baby's health, *senhora*.' A glass was pushed into her hand. 'We call this a *caipirinha*—*cachaça* mixed with mashed lemon slices, sugar and ice. Most foreigners enjoy it.'

'Thank you.' She smiled at her informer. 'I'm not exactly a foreigner, but it certainly looks marvellous.' She took a long draught of the fiery white rum mixture, feeling it surge through her blood like a naked flame. Where on earth could Rico be?

A sudden commotion a few yards away momentarily distracted her. Moving towards it she saw one of the young *gauchos* throw a long wooden pole on to the ground, and, with an arrogant smile at a very pretty girl standing nearby, take up a stance to one side of it. Immediately he was joined by another cowboy, similarly attired in cotton shirt, coarse body-fitting trousers and high, leather-spurred boots, who took up a position on the other side of the pole. The music which had lulled started again in earnest as the two men began to dance, and Sable found herself carried forward by the watching crowd.

As the music grew wilder the steps of the two men grew faster and more intricate, displaying a gymnastic ability which Sable found breathtaking.

'It's called the *chula, senhora*.' The man who'd given her the drink was again at her side. 'In the long nights on the range with nothing to do, our *gauchos* dance it as a duel rather than fight with knives or whips.' He smiled at her astonishment. 'It's a way of settling arguments without bloodshed. The onlookers judge the performance on ability; a winner is chosen and honour is satisfied. We believe the more highly motivated a man is, the better his performance, thus the outcome is fair.'

'They're both magnificent!' Sable was honestly admiring, as the original challenger performed an incredible leap, the crowd roared their approval, the music came to a sudden end, and the watching girl drew a crimson flower from her hair, tossing it at the winner's feet.

'But not as good as the *senhor*, your husband,' came the surprising reply. 'If you want to see how the *chula* may be danced, you should ask him to perform it for you.'

Nothing would have pleased her better, Sable thought grimly. Rico had to be somewhere. After all, he'd said it was his duty to attend! Then, suddenly, she saw him, seated at a table, his back towards the party, in deep conversation with a group of men. So much socialising!

'Why not?' she excused herself with a smile determination. The winner of the previous contest was still seeking a challenger, the flower from his admirer jauntily arrayed in a buttonhole of his shirt, as she approached Rico and laid her hand on his shoulder. When she'd come here she'd had no idea how she was going to stimulate Rico into abandoning his attitude of noble self-sacrifice, and resurrect the passionate, demanding man she'd grown to love . . . Only that she had to try. Now she'd been given the opportunity she'd sought . . .

'Sable—what the . . .' He was on his feet, frowning. 'I told them you were unwell.'

'And I told them I was better!' She faced him boldly. 'Why shouldn't I be here?'

'Because you don't belong . . .' He thrust his fingers through his dark hair as he saw the hurt look in her eyes. 'What I mean is, you'll be leaving soon. It's not right to raise their expectations.'

Well, she wasn't going to argue the niceties of that point now. There were other ways of gaining her ends.

'I want you to dance the *chula* for me,' she told him coolly. 'I'm told you're quite an expert.'

'For God's sake, Sable, have you no understanding?' he asked harshly. 'Can't you see I'm in no mood for dancing?'

'Force yourself.' She stood before him, eyes flashing, hands on hips, daring him to refuse her. 'Where's your spirit, Rico? Or do I have to find another champion?'

Terrified by her own audacity, she dragged her arm away from his angry grasp as he grated, 'What exactly do you mean by that?'

Running from him, her shaking fingers pulling her bright ear-rings from their anchorage, she tossed them down on the makeshift arena.

'Who will dance for me?' Her voice rang out proud and strong, to be followed by a sudden hush as the onlookers exchanged embarrassed glances.

'I think they are all too tired, *senhora*,' the young man sporting the flower suggested awkwardly. 'And I could use a drink myself.' He bent down, retrieved the pole and reached for the ear-rings.

'Leave them.' Rico's voice, cool and masterful, brooked no argument as he shouldered his way through the crowd, and, reaching out, took the pole, flinging it to the ground with purposeful strength. An uplifted arm commanded the music to play—and the duel of dance began.

All her life Sable would remember it. The blackness of the Brazilian night, the warmth of the flickering fires, the breathless attention of the crowd and the two men locked in a duel of movement and dexterity as serious as if their lives depended on it. But it was *her* life, *her* future that depended on the outcome and what would follow. She could only watch and pray that her plan would work.

She'd gambled on the information about Rico's prowess being true, added to her own experience of his ability on a dance-floor—and she'd won. Both men were drenched in sweat, their breathing laboured, when by unanimous applause Rico was declared the winner.

With one final lithe movement he swept his hand towards the ground, secured the scarlet baubles she'd flung there, and walked purposefully towards her, taking her unresisting arm, guiding her through the crowd which parted to make way for them, not stopping until they were beyond the circle of light and noise.

Held captive against some indeterminate farm building, pinioned into place by Rico's vibrantly aware body, Sable savoured the joy and excitement of his urgent possession of her mouth. Hands that trembled—excitement or exertion?—travelled a path of sensuous delight over every inch of her body, slipping the neck of her dress aside, they caressed the soft skin of her shoulders, found their way unhindered to her breasts, drifted towards her hips, cajoling, adoring . . . There was no need for words as Rico paid homage to her beauty, acknowledging his desire, his mouth hot and fervent, the virile thrust of his body claiming her for his own.

Somehow Sable managed to thread her slender hands between their compressed bodies, discovering the buckle of the low-slung belt that encased Rico's hips, breaking it open and reaching her fingers beneath the revealed waistband to explore the firm, warm flesh beneath it.

She felt the hard muscles beneath her hands clench as his skin shivered to her touch.

'Do you know what you're doing to me?' It was an agonising groan, husky with passion. 'Are you mad? Do you want me to take you here . . . now?'

'No!' She felt him stiffen, felt the surge of

disappointment flood through him, and knew he'd misunderstood. Quickly she continued, 'No, not here, *meu amor*, I've lost my appetite for public performances, but there's a perfectly good bridal bed waiting for us . . .'

'Dear God, Sable—is this some kind of revenge?' He was holding himself under magnificent control, and she couldn't find the heart to tease him. Besides, to delay matters further would only add to her own torment.

'No revenge, *meu amor* . . .' Every pore of her skin, every cell of her body surged with joy as she made her sweet confession. 'I love you too, Rico . . . oh, so much. I only realised how much after I left you, and then it was too late to tell you . . . I thought you hated me.'

'Love? You *love* me, Sable, despite everything?' He shook his dark head wonderingly, as if he was witnessing a miracle. 'I can't . . . I daren't believe it!'

She heard the break in his deep voice and her heart swelled with joy and pride because she had the power to change his disbelief into reality.

'Then let me show you,' she offered softly. 'Let me show you, Rico.'

In the bedroom she knelt at Rico's feet, drawing the leather riding boots from the man who was at last to become her lover. The small service completed, she was lifted into his arms, laid with tenderness on the soft coverings of the bridal bed. Each movement he made to divest her of the simple clothes that hid her total beauty from him was made with loving care.

His lower lip caught between his teeth, his dark eyes worshipping her, his laboured breathing and trembling fingers speaking as loudly as the soft endearments he whispered against her skin, Rico prepared his bride to receive his body and with it the declaration of his fidelity and support for as long as they both should live.

'Rico . . .' Sable whispered his name through lips swollen with passion, aching to receive him, her body ripened for love by his tender consideration. 'There's one thing you should know.' Even on the brink of no return he paused. 'Simon . . .' She felt him tense, could almost feel the pain she'd caused him, and hastened to continue. 'Simon lied to my father. We were never lovers—and I never wanted to pretend we were . . .'

'Isabella . . .' There was wonderment and joy in the lustrous eyes that held her own gaze.

'You see, I'm truly my father's daughter, after all.' Her smile was all woman, all love as she offered herself unrestrainedly to his seeking body. 'I was waiting for a man who would love me as much as I love him . . . and I believe I've found him.'

'Oh, yes, *minha querida* . . . oh, yes!' It was a shout of triumphant possession, and afterwards there was no need for words, as the phantom cowboy of the plains discovered his own true love at last, and the errant daughter claimed her heritage as his woman and discovered the experience sweet.

A long time afterwards, as they lay, their limbs entwined in happy exhaustion, Rico's fingers drifted caressingly down Sable's arm. 'It won't be possible to be mistress of Ribatejo and a cabaret artiste as well,' he murmured softly. 'What if you grow to resent me for coming between you and your heart's desire?'

'Silly.' She turned her head slightly and trailed her lips across his firm tanned shoulder. '*You* are my heart's desire. Besides, I realise now that I was only looking for the love and admiration I thought had passed me by.'

'And now?' He smiled down fondly at her.

'I realise that my father's never stopped loving me and I have your love as well and . . .' She paused delicately.

'And?' Rico prompted softly, turning to gaze down into her eyes.

'Well, in time there will be our children to love me, too . . . won't there?'

'Oh, yes, *meu amor*, oh, yes!' Rico's mouth sought hers, and as she felt her whole body quiver into expectant life, Sable knew that for her a whole life of love was just beginning.

Harlequin Presents

Coming Next Month

1183 HEAT OF THE MOMENT Lindsay Armstrong
Serena's first encounter with Sean Wentworth is embarrassing—so she's surprised to get the job of looking after his nephews at his remote Queensland station. Her relationship with Sean is just beginning to blossom when the past catches up with her.

1184 TRUE PARADISE Catherine George
If Roberto Monteiro chooses to think Charlotte used her female charms to gain her own—or her father's—ends, let him. Once he leaves the neighborhood she needn't see him again. Then Roberto insists that Charlotte come to Brazil with the contract....

1185 STORMY ATTRACTION Madeleine Ker
Paula prepares to do everything she can to keep the small island paradise off Majorca from development. She hadn't known her opponent would be charming Juan Torres—or that her heart would be at war with her convictions!

1186 THE THIRD KISS Joanna Mansell
Separated from her holiday group in Egypt, Bethan is rescued by Max Lansdelle. Only after she blackmails him into letting her stay in his camp does she realize that Max is not the cool customer she thought he was.

1187 PRISONER OF THE MIND Margaret Mayo
Lucy blames arrogant businessman Conan Templeton for her father's death and is horrified when she has to act as his secretary. So why is she disappointed when theirs seems likely to remain only a business relationship?

1188 A QUESTION OF LOVE Annabel Murray
Keir Trevelyan finally tracks down his dead brother's child, but Venna isn't going to give up her half sister's daughter that easily. She pretends to be a reckless mother with loose morals. Naturally, she's trapped by her own deception....

1189 WHITE MIDNIGHT Kathleen O'Brien
Amanda is desperate to be rid of Drake Daniels when he invades her family's Georgia estate, flaunting his new wealth. She once gave him everything—and paid the price.

1190 A DIFFERENT DREAM Frances Roding
Lucilla Bellaire wants success and is prepared to go to any lengths for it—or so she thinks. When Nicholas Barrington is neither bowled over by her beauty nor repelled by her ruthlessness, she faces a situation she can't cope with.

Available in July wherever paperback books are sold, or through Harlequin Reader Service:

In the U.S.
901 Fuhrmann Blvd.
P.O. Box 1397
Buffalo, N.Y. 14240-1397

In Canada
P.O. Box 603
Fort Erie, Ontario
L2A 5X3

Have You Ever Wondered If You Could Write A Harlequin Novel?

Here's great news—Harlequin is offering a series of cassette tapes to help you do just that. Written by Harlequin editors, these tapes give practical advice on how to make your characters—and your story—come alive. There's a tape for each contemporary romance series Harlequin publishes.

Mail order only

All sales final

TO: *Harlequin Reader Service*
Audiocassette Tape Offer
P.O. Box 1396
Buffalo, NY 14269-1396

I enclose a check/money order payable to HARLEQUIN READER SERVICE® for $9.70 ($8.95 plus 75¢ postage and handling) for EACH tape ordered for the total sum of $_____*
Please send:

☐ Romance and Presents   ☐ Intrigue
☐ American Romance   ☐ Temptation
☐ Superromance   ☐ All five tapes ($38.80 total)

Signature_____
                                                   (please print clearly)
Name:_____
Address:_____
State:_____ Zip:_____

*Iowa and New York residents add appropriate sales tax.

AUDIO-H

ANNOUNCING . . .

The Lost Moon Flower
by Bethany Campbell

Look for it this August
wherever Harlequins are sold